JOY AT MOONGLOW

JOY AT MOONGLOW

A Moonglow Christmas Novella

DEBORAH GARNER

CRANBERRY COVE PRESS

Cranberry Cove Press / Published by arrangement with the author

Joy at Moonglow by Deborah Garner

Cranberry Cove Press
PO Box 1671
Jackson, WY 83001, United States

Cover design by Mariah Sinclair | www.mariahsinclair.com

Library of Congress Catalog-in-Publication Data Available
Garner, Deborah
Joy at Moonglow / Deborah Garner—1st United States edition
1. Fiction 2. Woman Authors 3. Holidays

p. cm.
ISBN-13:
978-1-952140-23-5 (paperback)
978-1-952140-24-2 (hardback)

Printed in the United States of America
10 9 8 7 6 5 4 3 2

For my mother,
who always made holidays special for us.

ONE

Soft light flowed from many a window in Timberton, casting a warm glow across the evening landscape, backlighting the falling powder outside shops and bathing the snow-covered ground around residences. It created an aura of winter magic throughout the small Montana town and set the stage for the kind of Christmas holiday that both young and old yearned for: the making of memories, the fulfillment of dreams.

Mist stepped cautiously along the sidewalk, taking care to avoid icy patches. It wouldn't do to risk injury just as Christmas guests were about to arrive to spend the holidays at the Timberton Hotel. There were meals to prepare, decorations to arrange, and a dozen other joyful tasks to be performed. Although many in the town contributed to the holiday activities, the primary responsibilities fell on Mist, resident artist and chef, along with Betty, the hotelkeeper. And they were lovingly embraced responsibilities, at that. Mist could think of no finer way to spend the holidays than making them special for those both near and far.

Arriving at the hotel's front entrance, Mist slipped inside and hung her cape on the coat stand. This was her habit now, established over the past year whenever she walked from the old Moonglow Café building, now renovated as a residence. Just a few doors down from the hotel, the location was perfect. And the brief stroll had become a type of meditation, a flowing of energy between her two favorite places. She often thought of the continual movement back and forth as reminiscent of an ocean wave, not unlike those she used to watch as a university student in Santa Cruz, California.

She passed through the café and into the kitchen, where she flipped the light switch on and set a kettle of water to boil on the stove. As she expected, Betty soon joined her, having anticipated Mist's arrival. Together, at the kitchen's center island, they would review the guest list together, just as they had for many years.

"Peppermint or ginger peach?" Mist set two teacups on the counter along with a sweetgrass basket of assorted herbal teas. "Or perhaps you'd prefer chamomile? I always find it soothing in the evening."

"Ginger peach for me, dear," Betty said. "That sounds deliciously like dessert, minus the calories." She laughed as she patted one hip, and Mist was reminded how much she adored the sweet senior.

Mist served the tea and added a plate of cranberry scones fresh from that morning. She started each day baking breads, muffins, or other tempting goods, filling the establishment with delightful aromas. Many appreciated this, especially those who stopped by early for coffee. Even when guests weren't staying at the hotel, locals knew they could find coffee in the lobby, often accompanied by some delicious type of freshly baked goods. For one thing, Clive, the owner of the local gem and art gallery as well as Betty's beau, could always be counted on to sneak in for the first cup of Java Love, as Mist called it. But there were others, many others who considered the hotel a home away from home.

"Who will we have as guests on this busiest of all Christmas years?" Betty smiled as she emphasized the word *busiest*. There was no question it was true. Mist's decision to be married on Christmas Eve had thrown a gauntlet of challenge upon the usual holiday activities, none of which Mist wanted canceled, especially the traditional Christmas Eve dinner in the Moonglow Café. Any attempts to suggest alternative dates for the wedding had been met with a smile and silence. All knew this to be Mist's way of replying with a firm no.

On top of everything, the town's Christmas Joy project, aiming to create a basket of treats for each family in the community, filled every second of spare time. Betty's traditional cookie exchange was also on the schedule.

Mist opened the registration book and perused the list of holiday guests, those who would be arriving over the next few days and staying through Christmas. "We only have a few new guests since all the regulars will be coming this year."

"Of course they will!" Betty chuckled. "They wouldn't miss it! And I don't mean the Christmas Eve dinner."

Mist nodded but didn't comment. She wasn't used to being the center of attention. But she wasn't that naive; this year would be different. Or would it? She took a sip of tea and pondered this. No, it would not be different. Although guests and locals might think so, the real essence of the holidays would be what it always was: the combined energies of people, the delight of sharing meals together, and the memories evoked by decorations, music, and camaraderie.

"Where did you go?" Betty quipped, having recognized the moment of pensive philosophy not uncommon for Mist.

"I was thinking how delightful it will be to have a full house and all the spirit of the holidays that goes along with that." Mist set the teacup down and focused on the registration book. "What a wonderful group we'll have this year. As you know, Clara and Andrew will be here as well as the professor. And I believe Michael will be here..." Mist smiled.

"I certainly hope so!" Betty exclaimed, laughing. "It might put a dent in the wedding celebration if the groom was absent. Who else?"

Mist ran her finger down the list of names, pausing at one line. "We have two sisters coming from Colorado."

"How nice!" Betty said. "I love the idea of sisters doing things together."

Mist nodded, causing a snowflake earring made from a beach shell to swing side to side. "Yes. I think these sisters may be in their seventies or so. Violet, the one who made the reservation, mentioned that they used to often take trips together decades ago. But they haven't in many years because her sister doesn't like to leave her house anymore, not since her husband passed away a few years ago."

"Then it's good she's bringing her," Betty said.

"Yes, despite the other sister trying to cancel the reservation. She called shortly after the first one."

"And yet didn't cancel?"

Mist took on an impish grin. "I told her the person who made the reservation would need to cancel it."

Betty mirrored Mist's grin. "Is this what we call a white lie?"

"Maybe a very pale white?" Mist suggested. "A wispy white, like chiffon or the spray above an ocean wave."

"And the first sister didn't cancel?"

Mist traced an invisible circle on the page several times. "They must have discussed it and decided to keep the trip."

Betty took a sip of tea and set her cup down. "Interesting, the way that came about."

"Christmas," Mist whispered. "'Tis the season of mysterious ways."

"I see." Betty nodded, leaning forward in an attempt to read the registration book. "Who else? You said we had guests coming from the east coast."

"Yes, from Virginia. They're bringing their children, ages five and nine. I believe the five-year-old is a girl and the nine-year-old is a boy."

"Children here for the holidays!" Betty clasped her hands and brought them to her chest. "That's always such a treat."

"I agree." Mist smiled as she closed the registration book. "It lets us see Christmas through the eyes of a child."

"A delightful way to look at the holidays." Betty finished her tea and looked at the kitchen clock. "I think I'll head over to the library to help with the Christmas Joy project. Millie and the others are planning to work late tonight." Betty stood and took her teacup over to the kitchen sink.

"I'm sure Millie will appreciate the help." Mist knew the town librarian would be grateful. The idea of preparing holiday baskets for Timberton's households had seemed ambitious when proposed earlier in the year. But the town vendors had welcomed the project with enthusiasm. Now, during the last few days before the planned Christmas Eve deliveries, many were working to bring the last details together.

Betty grabbed a jacket from the hook near the kitchen's side door and headed out for the short walk to the library. As she stepped outside and started down the sidewalk, Mist watched from the kitchen window. The anticipation of all to come was almost palpable.

Yes, it would indeed be the busiest of holiday seasons.

TWO

Every morning offered its own list of tasks— or opportunities, as Mist preferred to call them—to prepare for incoming guests as well as town activities. As such, the following morning was filled with the comings and goings of local townsfolk for coffee and a casual breakfast, phone calls from incoming guests to double-check directions to the hotel or to solicit help for the Christmas Joy project.

Mist occupied the postbreakfast time by setting up curried butternut squash soup on the stove to simmer. As the aromas of garlic, shallots, curry, and cinnamon wafted through the hotel, she retired to the small back room that she used as an art studio. There she added final touches to several miniature paintings she had promised Clive for his gallery. The paintings were a popular item, and Mist just barely kept up with the demand, especially around the holidays when scenes of pine cones, snowmen, winterberries, and mistletoe were in heavy demand. As something new for this year, she'd started a series with birds, having been inspired by a picture of a cardinal she'd seen at a recent photography exhibit. The bright red cardinal stood in striking contrast to the snow-covered evergreen branches that she painted around it. And the tiny, delicate claws resting on those branches delighted her.

Leaving the paintings to dry, she moved on to the closet she liked to think of as a treasure chest. It was here she stored trinkets, toys, and anything else she gathered during the year. She believed that whatever items she chose to put in each guest's room would somehow inspire them or perhaps bring back a memory. Having no knowledge of many of the guests before they arrived, she relied upon instinct for her selections.

Baskets, boxes, and bins greeted Mist as she opened the closet door and stepped inside. It was a large space, more the size of a walk-in wardrobe than a small storage area. Over the years, she'd accumulated a collection that some might call strange but Mist perceived as enchanting. Vintage toys mixed with modern pottery. An old fishing rod rested alongside a basket of delicate lace. Costume jewelry, foreign coins, buttons, and plush animals kept court with wooden puzzles, candleholders, feather boas, and old comic books.

Every year she acquired new items, which she tucked away for future use. This year she'd added a tiny china elephant, a not-so-tiny stained-glass window, a copy of *Life* magazine from 1957 that she'd found in a used bookstore, and a variety of other unusual and whimsical items. These she gathered along with bits and pieces from past finds and room by room distributed them in a random but intuitive fashion.

Mist had just clipped her hair back with a beaded barrette and returned to the kitchen when she heard the front door open and close. A moment later,

Maisie's welcome face poked itself inside the kitchen door. Mist smiled, happy to see the petite florist taking a break from work. Christmas orders had been especially heavy this year with the Christmas Joy project on top of usual holiday requests. Along with contributions from other businesses, Maisie's Daisies would be delivering festive arrangements of flowers and greenery to Timberton households.

"How's it going over there at the shop?" Mist held out a spoonful of the soup for Maisie to taste, cupping her hand below the spoon.

"Mmm," Maisie murmured after taking a sip. "Delicious! It's going okay. Sally and Glenda are both helping. We've made thirty-two arrangements already today. That makes eighty-six altogether, counting the fifty-four we made yesterday." She crossed the kitchen and took a clean spoon from a drawer. With a sly smile, she dipped it into the pot of soup on the stove and took another taste. "I just had to make sure it was as delicious as the first spoonful."

"And?"

"Absolutely perfect," Maisie said, placing the spoon in the sink. "I wish I could stay, but we're trying to reach an even one hundred arrangements by tonight."

"I'll save some for you," Mist said. "And an individual loaf of olive bread too. You can eat it at the shop or take it home to Clay and Junior."

"Better save some for Marge as well. She's making her third batch of maple-nut fudge right now, aiming for fifty cellophane-wrapped packages to add to the project offerings."

"Those will be well received, I'm sure," Mist said. "Marge's fudge is wonderful."

"Just like her caramels," Betty added, stepping into the kitchen. Her comment caused both Mist and Maisie to smile. If there was one thing Betty was known for, it was her addiction to caramels. The hidden stash she kept in a drawer at the registration counter was hardly a secret.

"And the peppermint bark she makes during the holidays. I keep a supply of that behind the counter at the shop," Maisie said, referring to Maisie's Daisies, source of all things floral. "I can't keep it at home, or Clay Jr. will find it and end up on a sugar high."

"He does have a sweet tooth, doesn't he," Betty mused. "I recall having to move the bowl of glazed cinnamon nuts out of his reach more than once. Speaking of which…" She scooted out of the kitchen and returned with a bowl only half-filled with the popular treats. Opening a canister of back stock she'd made a few days before, she filled the bowl up to the brim. Maisie grabbed a small handful, thanked Betty and Mist, and headed back to the activity at the flower shop.

"Perhaps I could use one too." Mist grinned as she helped herself to one of the sweet treats.

"What's on the agenda for today?" Betty set the bowl of glazed nuts on the counter and opened the registration book. "Everyone checking in?"

"Most everyone," Mist said. "Clara and Andrew won't be here until tomorrow. All the new guests are arriving today. And Michael and the professor should be here anytime. At least they said they'd be here today... or was it tomorrow?" Mist stirred the soup, trying to recall the last conversation she had with Michael. "Honestly, now I can't recall. Where is my mind lately?"

Betty laughed. "I imagine quite occupied! I'm surprised you can keep anything straight. Maybe your nerves are acting up."

"I don't think so." Mist thought about that statement as she heard herself say the words. It wasn't in her nature to be nervous about much of anything. She didn't feel shaky or fidgety or worried. No, her nerves were fine.

"Yet you're not sure when your future husband said he'd be here," Betty pointed out. "That might be an important detail this week." She chuckled.

Mist set the soup spoon down on the counter and turned the burner to a low simmer. "*That* he'll be here, yes, I can see that's important. *When* he'll be here? That's up to him. You know how I feel about time."

As tended to happen, Clive's voice popped up out of nowhere, just in time to toss Mist a bit of her own philosophy. "Yes, time is flexible. Time is fluid. There is no future. The future is always now."

"Yes, dear." Betty rolled her eyes. Mist simply smiled, quite used to Clive teasing her about her new age perspective on life.

"I just stopped by for a cup of that fine Java Love you serve here." Clive, like many other townsfolk, had grown fond of Mist's own brew of coffee.

"But I'll take it to go, if you pretty ladies don't mind." Clive grabbed a mug and filled it from a coffeepot on the counter. "The future does seem to be now, according to the activity at the gallery today. Busy as all get-out with last-minute shoppers. Plenty of your miniature paintings selling as well as my custom jewelry."

A knock on the front door signaled an arrival. As if by prearranged agreement, Clive said a quick thanks and left out the side door. Betty and Mist started toward the lobby.

"Never a dull moment!" Betty exclaimed.

Indeed. Mist thought to herself. *And we wouldn't want it any other way.*

THREE

Though there was no need for guests to wait for entry, the Timberton Hotel resembled more of a house than a business from the outside, and it wasn't unusual for first-time visitors to err on the reserved side, hesitating at the entrance rather than letting themselves in.

Betty opened the door and stepped back as Mist greeted the two women on the front porch. Feeling the rush of cold air, Mist motioned them inside. Betty closed the door quickly and offered to take their jackets.

"You must be the sisters from Colorado," Mist said, reaching out to shake each woman's hand. "Violet and Rose, I believe."

The taller of the two nodded, introducing herself as Violet. Mist estimated her to be older by five or six years than her sister, who stood quietly by her side. Each woman wore a different jacket, both in earth tones, Violet's long and tan, Rose's shorter in a shade most resembling plum. As they removed their jackets, Mist noted their builds were different—Violet willowy with long legs that alone accounted for a good portion of her height, Rose more on the stocky side though not what one would call plump. Their mannerisms were unique as well. Violet moved with a silky smoothness, her arm reaching out gracefully as she handed Betty her jacket to hang on the coat tree in the corner of the foyer. She came across as self-assured yet not at all haughty. Rose, on the other hand, seemed an odd combination of reserved and skittish. Mist suspected Rose to be the sister who had tried to cancel the reservation.

"What a delightful hotel!" Violet said, taking in the surroundings and turning to her sister. "Don't you agree?"

Rose nodded obediently, looking around without comment.

"I'll set your registration card on the counter for you to fill out," Betty said, excusing herself. "Mist will help you get settled. I'm heading out to help with a community project."

"How lovely," Violet said. "What type of project?"

"Christmas baskets for the families here in Timberton," Betty said. "We call it the Christmas Joy project."

"Wonderful!" Violet exclaimed. "If you need help, let us know. We love helping with things like that, don't we, Rose?" Rose nodded timidly in agreement. Betty thanked the women and scooted out the door.

"It is indeed the season of giving," Violet said.

"As is every season," Mist said softly. The statement might have sounded patronizing by anyone else, but coming from Mist, it came across as sweet and sincere, just as intended.

Violet filled out the registration card while Rose peeked into the front parlor.

"Do you have luggage?" Mist asked, glancing at the floor and not seeing any. "I'll be glad to help you with your bags."

"They're in the back of our rental car," Violet said. "We thought we'd get settled in first. We'll bring them in later."

Mist nodded. "That's fine. If you'd like help then, just let us know." She took two keys from one of multiple hooks behind the counter and turned back to the two women. "Why don't I show you to your room? It's a favorite of mine with lovely light and comfortable chairs for relaxing and reading." She extended an arm, indicating the staircase, and together the three climbed to the second floor.

Arriving upstairs, Mist opened the door to a spacious suite. It was the accommodation she liked to give families or guests traveling together. Separate bedrooms stood to each side of an entry room that served as a small sitting area. This allowed guests to spend time together as well as to have the privacy of individual rooms.

"It's charming!" Violet exclaimed as she looked around. Mist followed her gaze, noting that she took in both the space and decor as well as a basket of trinkets from the downstairs closet. Mist had gathered the odd variety of items—miniature china horses, oversized buttons, marbles, and old postcards—into a sweetgrass basket, which lay on a cherrywood table in front of an antique camelback sofa.

"I'll let you get settled in," Mist said. "There's coffee, tea, and hot apple cider in the lobby as well as some glazed cinnamon nuts. And we'll be serving a casual dinner in the Moonglow Café tonight, just off the lobby."

"For hotel guests?" Violet replied. "That's wonderful."

"For the whole town, really," Mist noted. "For anyone who stops by."

"How on earth do you manage that?" Violet exclaimed. "The whole town? This building must be bigger than it looks from the outside!"

Mist smiled. "Not everyone comes every night, and not everyone comes at the same time. And it's a small town."

"So it works out," Violet mused.

"Yes," Mist said, "whether by chance or by magic. Most likely some of each." She stepped into the hall, leaving the guests with a final comment. "I hope you'll be able to join us, but please know that this is your home for the holidays. You're welcome to spend each moment as you wish."

Returning downstairs, Mist made herself at home in the kitchen, reminded of the evening meal. Not many townsfolk were expected for dinner. Many had family visiting from out of town, and others had gone off to larger towns for last-minute Christmas shopping. Still others made a point of eating at home on the days leading up to the legendary dinner served at the Timberton Hotel on Christmas Eve. That event had become so popular that—in spite of Mist's desire to have an unscheduled ebb and flow to all aspects of life—the meal was offered by reservation, with two seatings.

For this reason, the meals served prior to Christmas Eve were purposely kept simple and sometimes even whimsical, depending on Mist's mood. People never knew what to expect when they came to the Moonglow Café. There were no menus, not even prices. Those who participated paid "what their hearts told them," according to the policy Mist set when she first arrived in Timberton. In the same manner, they could eat what appealed to them and skip what didn't appeal to them—a circumstance that was extremely rare considering the exquisite food to be found on the buffet on any given evening.

These simple dinners were the reason Mist had set the butternut squash soup to simmer earlier. Soup was easy to prepare in advance and always well received on a chilly night. And for those not looking for something to warm them, the olive bread she'd promised Maisie could accompany a fresh spinach salad with pomegranates and a balsamic vinaigrette along with a selection of fresh fruits and cheeses. It was simple and yet varied, just what the evening called for.

Mist moved into the café to check that everything was in order. Knowing this would be an especially busy holiday, Mist had decided—somewhat hesitantly, as she loved arranging fresh flowers—to create dried flower arrangements for the table centerpieces this year, which she'd finished weeks earlier. She regarded them now, pleased with the touch of Christmas spirit that they added to each table. The combination of white-tipped lodgepole pine cones, eucalyptus, faux red berries, and wire-edged silver ribbon looked festive.

Reassured that the evening's meal was under control, Mist returned to the kitchen to wait for the next guests to arrive.

FOUR

Mist was rummaging through her favorite produce basket for shallots when she felt a soft kiss on the back of her neck. She smiled and, just to be impish, pretended she didn't feel anything. She continued to sort through vegetables as another kiss followed, and yet another, slowly moving around to the side of her neck. Finally, unable to hold back the laugh that had been threatening to escape since the soft lips first brushed against her skin, she spun around.

"Well, that's better!" Michael said, teasing. "I was beginning to think you'd grown immune to my charms."

"Never," Mist said, two shallots in one hand and a large, unwieldy vegetable in the other. She leaned forward to accept a proper kiss. "When did you arrive? And how did you manage to sneak up on me like that?"

"As for your first question, just a few minutes ago. I drove down from Missoula with the professor. As for the second, it appears vegetables are far more intriguing than I ever imagined." Michael looked questionably at one of her hands. "What is that anyway?"

"I was just about to ask the same thing," a familiar voice said from the kitchen door. Over Michael's shoulder, Mist smiled at the welcome sight of Nigel Hennessy, better known to all as the professor.

"This is a rutabaga," Mist said, delighted to show up the knowledge of two university teachers combined. If they could quote Shakespeare lines, she could quote root vegetable specifics. "Similar to a turnip, but larger. They're both from the cabbage family, though turnips are generally a summer crop while this fine specimen here prefers the winter." She raised the rutabaga in the air to show it off.

"I dare say, is that something we'll be expected to eat?" the professor said, his British accent making his question sound marginally more serious than it was, his hint of a smile making it less so.

"Perhaps..." Mist looked at the round object quizzically. "I might roast some with thyme and brown sugar. I haven't decided yet."

"I see," the professor said, adjusting the glasses on the bridge of his nose. "Well, if you cook it, I'll jolly well eat it."

"That's the spirit." Mist tossed the rutabaga in the air, catching it easily on its return and sweeping it into the basket. She dropped the shallots in as well and turned her attention to the sound of incoming guests. "I'd better get out to the lobby. Betty's over at the library, helping Millie. I don't want to keep people waiting." She excused herself, leaving Michael and the professor on their own. Nigel knew where his room was after so many years—eight that she could count—and Michael would likely head to their new house down the street.

As expected, the newest arrivals were the Sadlers, the family from Virginia. The father, Burton, was tall and lean with a shock of brown hair and a serious stance. He nodded hello but did not speak or smile. Elaine, the mother, was as pleasant and outgoing as her husband was reserved. She greeted Mist enthusiastically and proceeded immediately to introduce both children: Hannah, a waif of a six-year-old girl with an air of mischief and a twinkle in her eye, and Alex, her nine-year-old brother, who struck Mist as a miniature of his father in both appearance and countenance.

"Welcome to the Timberton Hotel," Mist said as she gestured to the bowl of glazed cinnamon nuts, a silent request for permission to offer them to the children. Getting an affirmative nod from Elaine, she lifted the dish off the counter and held it low enough for Hannah to reach. Alex, in keeping with his serious countenance, waited until the bowl was at a more proper level for his height.

"Sweet like cotton candy but crunchy!" Hannah chirped. She reached for another glazed nut, but Elaine suggested waiting until after dinner. Hannah agreed and withdrew her hand. Mist reassured the young girl that they would be there after the evening meal.

Burton filled out the registration card in an efficient, no-nonsense manner and pushed it forward on the counter. Making quick eye contact with Mist, he asked if they could be shown to their room.

"Right this way," Mist said, gesturing at the staircase. "Would you like any help with your luggage?" Four suitcases, three larger than the fourth, which had a small, plush unicorn dangling from its handle, sat by the front doorway.

"Thank you, but we can manage," Burton said. He took two of the larger suitcases, Elaine took the other large one, and Alex took the smallest.

"I can carry that one, Alex," Elaine offered.

"He's fine, Elaine," Burton said. "That's Hannah's bag. It barely weighs anything."

"I suppose so," Elaine said, her expression half agreement and half what Mist perceived to be resignation.

Mist ushered them to the second floor and down to the end of the hallway, opening the door to a spacious room with a queen-sized bed and sitting area. Sunlight flowed in through a large picture window, giving the room a light, airy ambiance. Before either parent had a chance to question the sleeping arrangements, Mist opened a door near the sitting area, indicating a second room with two twin beds. "I know you requested two roll-away beds, but this room is not being used, and I thought it would be more comfortable for you as a family."

"Oh, this is wonderful!" Elaine exclaimed. "How perfect!"

"Our own room!" Hannah skipped through the interior door, delighted with the arrangement. She eyed both beds and hopped up on one, claiming it as her own. Alex followed, more reserved but clearly pleased. He set the suitcases down and claimed the second bed.

"This will be fine," Burton said as if there'd been any question to begin with. He set the remaining luggage down by a closet and thanked Mist for her help. Taking this as a cue, she informed them of the basic hotel amenities, including the complimentary dinner in the café, should they choose to join others. She then returned downstairs, where she found Michael still in the kitchen.

"Did the professor head up to his room?" Mist asked, noting his absence.

Michael nodded. "Yes. He said he needed to check to see if you'd remembered his tea. He was kidding, of course."

"As if I would forget after all these years." Mist laughed. "In fact, he's in for a surprise. I picked up an electric kettle for his room so he can have hot water anytime he wants. I still gave him his favorite teacup and teapot though. I know better than to break tradition."

"Smart girl," Michael said. "He *is* a creature of habit, our professor."

Mist smiled. "Yes, he is. One of many reasons we love him."

FIVE

The evening meal brought in a larger crowd than Mist had anticipated. But she always prepared enough to feed more diners than she expected. Extra food never went to waste. A refrigerator in a downstairs room that the formerly homeless town resident, Hollister, stayed in always stood ready to take on a few servings. In addition, both Mist and Betty had been known to bundle up packages to go home with customers when they left. There were always people who needed food, and amazingly, there was always food for those people. At least where the Moonglow Café was concerned.

Wild Bill, the owner of the local greasy spoon, was one of the first to arrive, accompanied by Sally from Second Hand Sally's thrift shop. A rumor had begun circulating around the town, a tale of budding romance between the two. No one was certain how true it was, but Wild Bill had always been a single diner before, and it did seem out of the ordinary for him to arrive with someone else.

Mist, while setting a ladle next to the soup tureen on the buffet, noticed Bill pulling a chair out for Sally to be seated. It was so out of character for the gruff, much-loved man that Mist had to turn her head to keep him from seeing her surprised grin. Yes, as rumors went, this one appeared to hold some truth.

"Did I see what I thought I saw?" Betty exclaimed, eyes wide, as Mist returned to the kitchen. She stood at the center island, filling baskets with sliced olive bread. "William Guthrie and Sally? My, my! Glenda and Marge have been whispering about this all week, but I didn't know if it was true."

"It could be," Mist said, a twinkle in her eye. "Christmas is a time for small miracles after all."

"Well," Betty said as she headed to the door with two bread baskets, "maybe Wild Bill isn't so wild. Maybe he can be tamed after all. You know, like I tamed Clive." She winked just before disappearing.

Mist barely had time to laugh before a new voice spoke up.

"What did she just say?" Clive stepped through the side door as Betty was exiting through the door to the café. "I only heard the last few words. Something about taming me?"

Mist tilted her head to the side. "Don't worry, that's not exactly the way I remember it. I recall you doing all sorts of chores around here, waiting patiently for Betty to notice and reciprocate your feelings. Didn't this go on for quite some time? Months? Years?"

"Decades," Clive admitted. "Oh, before I forget… can I get any more of your mini paintings for the gallery? For last-minute shoppers? And what's for dinner?" he added without missing a beat. "Better yet, what's for dessert?"

Betty chuckled as she returned to the kitchen. "Well, look who the dinner bell dragged in. Funny how this character shows up when there's food around." She gave Clive an affectionate peck on the cheek, grabbed two more baskets, and then ran the bread out to the café.

"I can bring a few more paintings down in the morning," Mist said, answering Clive. "As for dessert, it's chocolate-mint ice cream. If you make it through the butternut squash soup, spinach pomegranate salad, and olive bread first."

"I'd better get started then!" Clive patted his stomach with both hands and then ambled toward the dining room, passing Betty as she returned to the kitchen.

"A guest is asking for you at the café door," Betty said, an eyebrow raised as she spoke to Mist. "Mr. Sadler. I'm not sure if there's a problem or not. He looks serious."

Mist nodded. "I suspect he looks serious most of the time if not all the time." Remembering his demeanor at check-in, she hoped he hadn't found something unsatisfactory with the family's accommodations. "I'll see what he needs."

"What else can I do to help?" Betty asked, looking around.

"Nothing," Mist said. "All the food is out on the buffet, and the bowls are ready for ice cream when people finish. Have a seat and rest."

Exiting the kitchen, she found the Sadler family standing in the doorway to the café. As expected,

Mr. Sadler looked somewhat concerned—or perhaps just perplexed—while Elaine and the children surveyed the room eagerly.

"Would you like to join us?" Mist gestured toward a large table that offered four empty chairs. Millie and Marge occupied two of the other seats. Ernie, the night bartender at Pop's Parlor, the local watering hole, filled another seat. His most recent girlfriend—he tended to go through them rather quickly—sat beside him.

Mr. Sadler cleared his throat. "I wasn't sure if we should seat ourselves. There's not an empty table."

"We're all family here," Mist explained. "You're welcome to sit anywhere, but I suggest the four empty chairs would be best." Clive, sitting within earshot, coughed. Without even looking, Mist knew he was grinning. Admittedly, her comment, while spoken sweetly, had a touch of sarcasm to it, which was unusual for her. Perhaps she was a bit nervous after all.

"Thank you!" Elaine said. She began to usher the children toward the seats. Mr. Sadler simply nodded and then followed.

Violet and Rose arrived next, choosing a small table where they engaged in conversation, Violet doing most of the talking.

Mist welcomed the sisters, encouraged them to help themselves to the buffet, and returned to the kitchen, contemplating the small encounters.

"What is it?" Betty asked as she lined up bowls in preparation for serving dessert.

Mist retrieved an ice-cream scoop from a drawer and handed it to Betty. "I'm not sure. I can't quite put my finger on it. I just hope our holiday here this year will help lighten everyone's spirits. Every single one of them."

* * *

It was late in the evening, after dinner, after prepping for the next morning's breakfast, that Mist retired to her room off the back hallway. Despite having the new home just down the block, this room was a place she kept for herself. It was a sanctuary, a place to stay when the hotel was full and guests might need attention, and lately, a place to keep treasured items such as the vintage cedar chest that stood to the side of her easel and art supplies. For this held something dear to her heart: her wedding dress.

Mist reached into the chest and lifted out the cherished garment. She ran her thumbs over the stitched beading as her hands cradled the soft ivory fabric below. The dress had been a labor of love for many months, weaving silk, lace, and beads together into a treasure she would slip into just as Michael had slipped into her heart the first time she met him. Many had offered to help with the sewing or beading, but this was something Mist wanted to do herself, by hand, a little bit at a time, the creation of the dress more a prayer than a task.

She carefully lowered the dress back into the chest, taking care to let it fold softly back and forth, like a ribbon of wishes. She would take it out the following day and let it rest on a satin hanger, let any soft wrinkles fade away. For now, the cedar walls offered a sense of safety, both for the dress and the dreams that went with it.

SIX

Morning arrived, bringing a light snowfall that caused every window in the hotel to look like a snow globe scene. Mist set up the early-morning coffee in the foyer at six a.m. and then stepped out on the front porch to take in the peaceful scene. The air was cool, crisp, and fresh, and a barely detectable breeze carried within it a feeling of anticipation. Was this her own personal sense of things to come? It felt stronger than that, as if the combined holiday excitement of all those in Timberton hovered in the air. She took a deep breath and held it, absorbing the feeling of a community consciousness. Exhaling, she stepped back inside.

Knowing the day would be full—bordering on hectic some might say—Mist had planned a simple breakfast, engaging, on a whim, with the help of Michael. Although not one to spend time in the kitchen, he rose to the occasion as the master of bacon for the meal, frying applewood bacon strips as Mist prepared scrambled eggs. At least these were her version of scrambled eggs, considering the unexpected—though optional—addition of avocado, feta, sun-dried tomatoes, and tarragon.

Mist knew Clive and Clayton had a wager going over whether Wild Bill would be brave enough to try the eggs "a la Mist" or if he'd request them plain. Clive was certain the popular local would avoid anything fancy. Clayton, on the other hand, thought the gourmet style might win out. Were she a betting person, she'd be tempted to play it safe and vote for basic scrambled eggs. But William Guthrie had been pulling surprises lately, as evidenced by his seeming affection for Sally. It was quite possible he'd be adventurous and opt for the fancier dish.

The morning breakfast crowd came in small waves, allowing Mist and Michael to keep up with fixing individual plates, which Betty then delivered to the tables. Platters of melon slices and cinnamon scones on the buffet let those dining choose their own side dishes. Pitchers of orange, cranberry, and apple juice accompanied the fruit and baked goods, and the coffee flowed freely. Everyone appeared pleased with the meal, especially Clayton when Clive begrudgingly handed him a twenty-dollar bill. Whether Wild Bill had chosen the fancier eggs to impress Sally or out of genuine curiosity, Mist doubted anyone would ever know. Yet another Christmas mystery had surfaced.

As the meal wound down and townsfolk and hotel guests departed for the day's activities, Mist packed up the leftover breakfast food—bacon in particular as Michael had taken on the enthusiasm of a new sous-chef—and placed it in the downstairs refrigerator. She returned to the kitchen, finding Betty taking care of the breakfast dishes while attempting to convince Michael not to help.

"I told your sweetheart I didn't need help with the dishes," Betty said. "I know he offered to help Clive today."

"It's true," Michael admitted, setting down plates he had just brought in from the dining room. "He's expecting a rush of last-minute shoppers."

"Why don't you go on up to the gallery?" Mist suggested. "I'll help Betty finish and then see you there. I promised Clive more mini paintings." She crossed the room and gave Michael a kiss.

"I can take those for you."

Mist shook her head. "I still need to choose which ones to take from the extras I made before the holidays. And I need to prepare casseroles for tonight's dinner. I'll drop the paintings off after that on my way to the library. I told Millie I would stop by to see how the Christmas Joy preparations are going."

"Busy, busy!" Betty hummed the words as she dipped a plate into a sink of soapy dishwater.

"Whatever you both say. I'm no match for the two of you!" Michael exchanged another kiss with Mist and headed out.

Gathering ingredients from their appropriate places, Mist pulled together two large casseroles for the evening meal and took them downstairs to the second refrigerator. She returned quickly, a puzzled look on her face, which Betty quickly noticed.

"What is it?"

"I must be losing my mind," Mist said. "I just put a plate of bacon in that refrigerator, and it's gone."

"That's strange," Betty said. "Is Hollister down there?"

"I didn't see him."

"Maybe you put it in this fridge instead?"

"I don't think so. I clearly remember taking it downstairs." To make sure, Mist looked in the kitchen refrigerator. As expected, there was no sign of the bacon.

"It's a mystery," Betty said. "The mystery of the missing bacon."

"Quite," Mist mused. "One that will be solved in time, I suppose. But I do need to get up to the gallery. At least tonight's dinner is ready to pop in the oven."

Assured that people's appetites would be satisfied that evening, Mist selected a dozen of her miniature paintings to take to Clive. Wrapping them carefully to protect them from the winter weather, she donned a favorite burgundy cape, knit cap, and gloves, and stepped outside.

Snow flurries brushed against Mist's cheeks as she walked to the gallery. She welcomed the snow, knowing it set the ambiance that guests expected for a winter holiday. And it added a freshness to the air, almost a perceptible fragrance, a sense of things to come.

The gallery was bustling with last-minute shoppers when Mist stepped through the door. Clive was tied up with a young couple, likely explaining the background of a necklace that dangled from the woman's hand. The custom jewelry he designed showcased the area's well-known Yogo sapphires, unique to Montana. The soothing blue color of the stones—although sapphires are not always blue—often caught the interest of those passing through. Visitors might fall for a piece of jewelry to take home with them, or they could even search through gravel at a workshop table there in the gallery, looking for a stone of their own. It was a fun and educational activity, sometimes—but not always—resulting in a find that could be polished and used.

Mist looked around, noting how much the gallery had grown since she first arrived in Timberton. In addition to Clive's constant new jewelry designs, the gallery's reputation for art had spread over the years. Although Mist supplied some of the artwork that graced the gallery's walls—her miniature paintings in particular—other local artists displayed their creations there as well. Western images, wildlife scenes, and landscapes of all kinds often found their way home with those who stopped in. Newly added were a handful of small bronze sculptures by an artist who had recently moved to Timberton. With artwork circling in and out as new additions arrived and others were sold, there was always something to see at the gallery.

"I see you made it," Michael said as Mist approached the back desk. He reached for the batch of paintings she held. "Let me take those for you. Clive already has orders for a couple of them, and I can tag the others." He lifted a clipboard of orders off the desk.

"You've become quite the efficient retail worker." Mist teased him as she handed him the paintings. She knew that Michael's heart was dedicated to teaching. His local outreach program for the university had become extremely successful, creating a waiting list for students wishing to study in the small town.

Michael laughed. "I can't let myself get bored over the winter holidays."

"As if that could happen in Timberton!" Clive joined in, having finished with the jewelry customers. "Thanks for bringing the paintings in, Mist."

"I'll leave you two to handle the gallery fun," Mist replied. "I'm off to the library and then back to the hotel." She looked at the two men fondly, hesitating briefly before leaving as she realized how much they each brought to the spirit of the town.

"What is it?" Clive asked. He and Michael exchanged glances.

"Absolutely nothing," Mist said, smiling at their puzzled expressions. She turned toward the door and cast one last comment over her shoulder. "Everything is perfect."

SEVEN

The library was filled with joyous, exuberant voices when Mist arrived. Laughter and happy chatter filled the much-loved space as children hovered over a wide spread of watercolors, pastels, gel pens, and glitter. Small sheets of paper lay on tabletops, each lovingly attended to by an eager young artist.

"There's no lovelier music than the sound of children's laughter," Mist said as she greeted Millie, the town librarian.

"They're enjoying themselves," Millie agreed, glancing around at a scene that could only be described as cheerful chaos.

"It was a wonderful idea, having them write and decorate Christmas messages and poems," Mist said. "You come up with the most inspiring projects. This library is a community treasure. These will be a fabulous addition to the Christmas Joy project."

Millie nodded. "We should have enough for all the baskets. Some of the children have made four or five of them."

"Excellent." Mist clasped her hands together, picturing the wide variety of items each household would receive. "A great surprise for those receiving the assortments."

A petite girl of around seven years of age ran up to Mist and held up her paper. Glitter-accented candy canes surrounded the words CHRISTMAS IS A TIME FOR SWEETS.

"That's wonderful!" Mist exclaimed as she admired the artwork. "I love the design you've chosen to go with your Christmas thoughts."

"Thanks, Missmiss!" the young girl chirped as she turned away, skipping back to her table. Mist laughed, recognizing the unique nickname from times the child had come by the Moonglow Café for dinner with her mother. An early attempt to say "Miss Mist" had quickly fallen into the simpler form.

"Do you think she'll start calling you Mrsmrs after Christmas?" Millie's eyes twinkled as she referred to Mist's upcoming nuptials.

"I doubt it," Mist mused, pondering the question. "I suspect—and hope—I'll always be Missmiss to her. It's quite endearing."

A second child approached, a boy Mist estimated to be nine or ten. His paper featured a red truck—large enough to run into the wording—carrying a Christmas tree. A golden retriever sat next to the truck, a dog Mist recognized as one the boy walked sometimes. The words in the center read CHRISTMAS IS A TIME FOR FAMILY.

"I love the truck, and I especially love the dog," Mist said. "Pets are indeed family, aren't they?"

"My mom and dad are family," the boy said. "I just didn't have room to draw them."

"Well," Mist said, inspecting the drawing closely. "Maybe they're standing behind the truck, and that's why you can't see them."

"Yeah, maybe they are." The boy's expression brightened.

"Or they might be invisible," Mist whispered.

The boy's eyes grew wide, and he looked at the drawing with new enthusiasm. "That's it! They're invisible!"

"People can't be invisible," a new, young voice said. Mist turned to see Alex, Elaine, and Hannah standing beside him.

"How can you be sure?" Mist asked. Though tempted to smile, she kept a straight face. "If they're invisible, you wouldn't be able to see that they're not there."

Alex remained quiet, seeming to contemplate Mist's words. He then shrugged his shoulders and turned, surveying the room.

"Millie told me about this at dinner last night," Elaine said. "She invited us to stop by. I thought the children might enjoy being with others their own age."

"An excellent idea." Mist turned to both children. "Why don't we find a place for you to join in? Or simply to watch, if you prefer," she added quickly, seeing a hesitant look cross Alex's face. Escorting the children out to the tables, she found Alex a place next to the boy who had drawn the red truck, and for Hannah, a chair not far away, in a group with girls of a similar age.

Returning to Elaine, Mist indicated a small area that had been arranged for parents who wanted to remain while their children enjoyed the activity. Seeing Millie in the process of setting up a fresh pot of coffee to brew, they headed that way.

"I'm so glad you showed up," Millie said as Elaine approached. "It'll be good for your kids to mix with the others."

"Yes," Elaine said. "Especially Alex." She turned to Mist. "His best friend moved away a month ago, and he's been pretty down since then. Keeps to himself."

"Perhaps meeting other children here will remind him there are future friends to make," Mist said, her gaze wandering to the table where Alex was in the process of borrowing gel pens from the boy who drew the red truck. Both boys were laughing. "He looks open to it."

Elaine looked at Alex and nodded. "Yes, he does. That's the first time I've seen him laugh since his friend moved away. I'm relieved." She turned to Millie. "Thank you for inviting us."

"You're welcome!" Millie said. "A library is for everyone: travelers as well as townsfolk, the young as well as… well, the not so young." Millie, very much a senior, tapped her own shoulder and winked.

"And it's filled with adventures for all ages," Mist added. "That's one of the wonderful things about reading. In only a few minutes, a book can whisk you off to another world."

"Even at my age?"

Mist turned to see Hannah standing next to her, wide-eyed.

"Especially at your age!" Mist whispered. "Let me show you!" Guiding Hannah through the stacks, she arrived at a section of children's books and pulled one off the shelf. "Like this, for example. You never know what you might find inside a treehouse."

"The... Magic... Tree... House," Hannah said slowly as she read the title. "That sounds fun. I want to see what's inside the treehouse."

"Easily arranged, my treehouse explorer," Mist said. "We have an arrangement with the library to be able to check out books for guests. We can take this back to the hotel. Maybe you can relax and read by the Christmas tree after dinner."

"Good idea!" Hannah beamed. "I'll read it after dinner! Now I'm going to color another one of those papers." She skipped off, returning to the children's art area. Mist returned to the coffee area to check the book out with Millie's help.

"One for the road?" Millie smiled as Mist handed her the book.

"Yes," Mist said. "One of hundreds, likely thousands of books she will read during her lifetime. I can tell she has the gift of curiosity that will nurture a love for reading. It warms my heart to think of the adventures that await her."

"That's a wonderful thought," Millie said.

Conversation around coffee resumed as Elaine and Millie shared favorite book titles and authors. It wasn't long before Hannah returned, clutching a sparkling paper. She handed it to Mist, who read, "CHRISTMAS IS FOR READING." Bright, colorful drawings of books surrounded the words, randomly scattered around the page, each dusted with an abundance of glitter.

"This is lovely, Hannah!" Elaine said, admiring her daughter's artwork. "Should we take this back to the hotel?"

Hannah shook her head. "No. It's for the Christmas baskets, just like the ones everyone's making. Maybe I can make another one later to keep. Is that okay, Mist?"

"Absolutely," Mist assured her. "I have plenty of art supplies you can use. Perhaps I'll make one with you. Would that be all right?"

"Yes!" Hannah exclaimed. "That would be really great."

"Then we'll plan on that for this evening after dinner. Shall we?" Mist looked to Elaine, who nodded.

"Alex made one too," Hannah said. "But he didn't use any glitter, so it's not sparkly like mine."

"I see," Mist mused. "Well, art can be very different, one piece to the next."

"You mean sometimes it's sparkly, and sometimes it's not?"

Mist nodded. "I think it would be pretty boring if all art looked the same. Don't you?"

"*So very* boring!" Hannah smacked one hand against her forehead for emphasis, which caused Millie and Elaine to grin.

"Hannah tends to be a little dramatic at times," Elaine said, hugging her daughter and placing a sweet kiss on top of her head.

"She lives life to the fullest," Mist said. "It's a gift."

EIGHT

No matter how busy the holidays turned out to be, no one ever wanted to miss Betty's annual cookie exchange, and this year was no exception. It wasn't even the sugary treats themselves that brought people to the hotel, bearing batches of cookies and platters of similar holiday goodies. Certainly the thought of lush chocolate, vanilla, lemon, ginger, and peanut butter flavors helped lure participants as did the textures of royal icing, chopped nuts, and candy sprinkles. But it was tradition itself that topped the reasons the cookie exchange was always well attended. That and perhaps a chance to hear the latest scoop on town gossip—all well-meaning, of course.

There was also the draw of the containers provided each year, always unique and creative. This was Mist's only involvement with the event, knowing it to be near and dear to Betty, something she had established years ago and took pride in organizing herself. But Mist delighted in coming up with different containers each year that could be used to hold the mix-and-match variety of sweets that would go home with each person once everything had been shared. Regular participants had come to save the containers over the years, accumulating a collection to be reused or just enjoyed as is. Wooden boxes, glass jars, baskets, and small sleighs had all been used at one time or another. Nothing terribly fancy as they were meant to be functional, not just decorative. But each year was a little different, just as everything in Timberton was somehow unique each year.

Months before, while frequenting antique shops and thrift stores in surrounding areas, Mist came across a stack of four vintage pie plates on a late summer afternoon. Shallow and circular with lovely, fluted edges, they seemed destined for a special holiday use. She'd purchased them all and little by little added others as she came across them. By mid-November, she knew there were enough to use for the cookie exchange. Now, with intricate painted swirls of silver and gold around the outer glass, they waited at the end of the buffet in the Moonglow Café, ready to be filled with cookies and sweets.

Betty had donned a festive outfit for the occasion, a vivid red sweater in soft mohair, decorated with white and silver rhinestone-bedecked snowflakes and paired with black satin slacks. It was a touch more sophisticated than her usual fun Christmas sweaters, and she received immediate oohs and aahs from every person who arrived for the event.

"Where on earth did you get that sweater? It's fabulous!" Marge exclaimed as she entered with a tray of macadamia nut brownies. She balanced the tray in one hand while reaching out to stroke the soft yarn, approving.

"From me, of course!" Sally laughed as she stepped in right behind Marge with a double batch of ginger snaps. Marge rolled her eyes, knowing the town's thrift shop often received unique items. It only took a serious dose of good luck to be there right when the best items appeared. Betty had obviously been lucky the day that sweater showed up on the racks.

A parade of holiday sweets followed, arriving one by one, plate by plate. Gingerbread truffles, butter cookies, orange honey shortbread, and pistachio-cranberry bark all made their way to the central area where participants would gather assortments to take home. Glenda, from the Curl 'N' Cue, showed up with a batch of her own holiday biscotti as well as a plate of double-chocolate brownies from Millie, who was tied up with the Christmas Joy activity at the library but sent her regards along with the baked treats.

"I think this is the best variety we've ever had!" Betty exclaimed.

"You may be right," Marge said. "It's tempting to taste one of each right now."

"You wouldn't dare," Sally said, her tone hinting of reprimand.

Marge shrugged her shoulders and laughed. "Of course not! But a girl can dream, right?"

"Well, *I* might dare if no one else does!" Clara Winslow's voice eagerly joined the others. Betty turned to see the much-loved yearly guest standing in the doorway, along with her husband. Both held suitcases and looked enthralled with the display of cookies and treats.

"Clara! Andrew!" Betty exclaimed, rushing over to greet them. "How wonderful to see you!" She pulled Clara into a warm embrace, then Andrew into the same.

"It's wonderful to be here, just as it is every Christmas!" Clara exclaimed.

"And look at that green streak in your hair!" Betty stepped back to admire it. "Maisie will be so proud of you."

Clara laughed. "Just trying to be stylish for the holidays. What color is Maisie's hair this year anyway?"

"Some sort of magenta, I'd say, with a bit of gold. Last month it was orange for a Thanksgiving theme, blended in perfectly with the cornucopia floral arrangements she had at Maisie's Daisies." Betty stepped around the registration counter and grabbed the key to their room. "How was your trip?"

"Not bad," Clara said. "Some flight delays, nothing out of the ordinary. Holiday travel, you know. I don't expect it to be smooth sailing."

"Nothing that a few cookies wouldn't fix." Andrew cast a longing glance at the crowd surrounding the cookie event.

"Don't worry, Andrew," Betty said. "There'll be plenty for us later. I'm making an assortment, just like everyone else."

"Well, if a brownie or two fall in there by accident, I won't complain." Andrew sent another longing glance at the assortment of treats as Clara smacked his shoulder in mock reprimand.

Another voice added to the mix as Mist entered the room. "Clara and Andrew, welcome!" As typical of her manner of movement, her approach was silent in spite of wearing her usual work boots.

"There she is, our bride-to-be!" Clara stretched her arms wide and welcomed Mist into them. "We're so excited for you and Michael."

"Thank you, both of you," Mist said, feeling the warmth of Clara's hug. "It's so good to see you!"

"I agree, of course!" Betty exclaimed as she handed the room key to Andrew. "It wouldn't be Christmas without you two here."

"It wouldn't be Christmas without being here," Andrew said. "And we certainly couldn't miss *this* year." He winked at Mist.

"We're all so excited," Betty said, waving to another bearer of cookies coming into the hotel. She gestured in the direction of the cookie-exchange crowd to direct the newcomer and then turned back to Clara and Andrew. "I honestly think Mist is the calmest of us all."

"Is that true, Mist?" Clara asked, eyebrows raised. "Do you really feel calm? Not nervous at all? Even a little?"

Mist considered it, not for the first time. It was a question she'd heard often over the past few weeks, more frequently as the date grew closer. But nervousness wouldn't be the word she'd use to describe her feelings. She felt anticipation, excitement, wonder, enchantment, fascination, hope, and promise. Above all, she felt peace.

"I don't think so," Mist replied, quite sure this was accurate after careful contemplation.

Betty nodded. "I'm inclined to agree with Mist. At least I haven't noticed any pre-wedding jitters or cold feet, as they say." Another person entered for the cookie exchange, and Betty excused herself to accompany a platter of butterscotch blondies into the main event.

"Why don't I let you get settled," Mist suggested. "You have your usual room upstairs. Coffee, tea, and Betty's glazed cinnamon walnuts can be found in the usual places."

"We'll certainly need a few of those!" Clara exclaimed. She turned to Andrew, who handed her the key to the room and lifted their suitcases. Turning down an offer from Mist to help with their luggage, they started up the hotel's staircase, and Mist headed to the kitchen, a dozen tasks waiting.

NINE

While it was true, as she had told Clara and Andrew, that she wasn't nervous, that assessment had been directed specifically toward the wedding, not the overall holiday festivities. When it came to everything that needed to be done over the next twenty-four hours, Mist admitted—at least to herself—to be feeling a touch of apprehension. This she categorized as a lower level of discomfort than nervousness would be. It simply amounted to knowing the list of tasks to be completed was a long one, and the time available to complete them was minimal.

Mist had barely started spreading supplies out on the kitchen island when a sweet giggle floated through the air. She looked around, curious where it had come from, and then wisely lowered her gaze to a child's height. Although the room was empty, a wiggling nose caught her eye, barely visible on the other side of the kitchen door, she quickly resumed arranging the item before her.

"What tiny fairy speaks to me?" Mist mused aloud. "So small it cannot be seen, so sweet it must be a dream!" For dramatic effect, she inhaled and exhaled slowly, which was promptly echoed by another giggle.

"Ah, if only it were a real fairy," she continued, "I would have the help I need to put together these hot cocoa packets." She sighed as she snuck a furtive glance at the door. "I'll just have to do it all by myself…" Another giggle. And then another. And then a burst of energy as Hannah threw open the kitchen door and hopped inside.

"I can help! I can be your fairy!"

Mist smiled at the young girl's enthusiasm. She had planned to put the packets together quickly on her own, but when unexpected opportunities like this came along, she believed in following them. This was a chance for her to get to know Hannah better as well as a chance for the child to build a Christmas memory. As for the task itself, it was bound to take twice—if not three times—as long, but it would be worth it.

"Oh, thank goodness!" Mist exclaimed. "I'm so glad to have a special helper. I thought I was going to have to make these all by myself."

"Help me up," Hannah said, more an eager command than a question. She patted a counter stool with one hand, and Mist helped her up. She made sure the young girl was steady in her seat, and then she prepared to explain the challenge before them, starting with a large canister.

"What's in there?" Hannah asked before Mist had a chance to speak.

"This…" Mist waved her hand above the container as a magician might signal the beginning of a magic trick. "This is a special blend of cocoa and powdered sugar with just a dash of salt."

"What's it for?"

"It's for people to mix with milk or water to make hot cocoa. We're delivering Christmas Joy baskets to families on Christmas Eve. This will be part of their gift." Mist picked up a small, compostable cellophane bag from a pile of many and retrieved a tablespoon from a utensil drawer. "We're going to fill these with the cocoa mixture."

"With that spoon?" Hannah asked.

Mist pretended to contemplate this. "Unless you brought your magic wand with you."

Hannah shrugged. "I left it at home."

"I see." Mist nodded thoughtfully. "Then I think we can make the spoon work. Let's try it." She opened the canister and filled a spoon. "We need three of these in each bag. How would you like to hold the bag open? If you hold it carefully and press in on the sides, I'll be able to put the cocoa mix in."

Hannah took the bag and followed Mist's directions, holding the bag open carefully. Mist dropped a spoonful of mix inside and then added two more.

"Three in each bag?" Hannah asked.

Mist nodded. "That's our recipe."

"Now what?" Hannah said, eyeing the bag of cocoa mix. Mist pointed to a tray on the counter. "Now we set the bag down carefully and fill another one. Later we'll put ribbons on the bags to hold them together."

Hannah placed the bag gently on the tray and picked up an empty bag. "Ready," she said.

Mist again placed three spoonfuls of cocoa mix in the bag, and Hannah set it next to the first bag.

Working together, they filled several more, and then Hannah informed Mist it was her turn to spoon the mix into the bags. Not one to dampen any child's enthusiasm, Mist relinquished the spoon, picked up an empty bag, and held it out while Hannah scooped the cocoa mix from the bowl. The first spoonful landed perfectly in the bag. Half of the second one made it into the bag while the other half spilled onto the counter. The third spoonful managed to fall into equal thirds: one portion in the bag, another portion on the counter, and a third portion on one of Mist's wrists.

Hannah sighed. "Maybe we'd better switch back."

Mist agreed but only after tapping her cheek as if pondering the suggestion, which caused the cocoa on her wrist to poof into the air and fall to the ground. Hannah giggled, and Mist smiled.

"I think you have a good idea." Mist moved the stack of plastic bags, and the two resumed the task. When the tray was full, Hannah held each bag up again as Mist tied a ribbon around the top, gathering the cellophane together.

"Well, look at that!" Betty exclaimed as she entered the kitchen with a plastic-wrapped pie plate of assorted sweets. "You two have been working hard while we were finishing up the cookie exchange."

"We made hot cocoa bags. I helped a lot!" Hannah beamed.

"I can see that!" Betty smiled as she set the cookie assortment on a side counter. "Mist is certainly lucky you came along to help. She's very busy this week. In fact, do you want to know a secret?" Hannah nodded eagerly, and Betty tiptoed over to whisper in her ear. Mist watched as Hannah's eyes grew wide. "Really?" She jumped off the stool and threw her arms around Mist. "You're getting married!" she shouted before jumping back and slapping her hand over her mouth. Removing it slowly, she whispered, "Does anyone else know?"

Betty and Mist both laughed. "Yes," Mist said. "You don't have to keep it a secret. It's not a surprise."

"Are you going to wear a beautiful dress?" Hannah's eyes beamed.

Mist nodded. "I do have a very pretty dress to wear. I made it with fabric and beads and lace that I collected over time."

"You made it? A whole wedding dress? Wow! Do you have something to wear on your head? Do you have flowers? Do you have a big cake?"

Mist smiled. "I do think I have all of that. Except…" She looked at Betty and then back at Hannah with eyes wide. "I forgot something!"

"What?" Hannah looked distraught, as if the fairy-tale wedding she'd just envisioned had collapsed. "What did you forget?"

"I forgot to find a flower girl!" Mist sent a pleading look at Betty. "What should I do? How can I get married without a flower girl?"

Betty shook her head, playing along. "I don't know. A wedding won't be the same without a flower girl. Maybe you'll need to cancel it and get married another time."

"Wait!" Mist stood. "I have an idea. Can you two wait right here? I'll see if my idea can work. If you wait, you can be the first to know."

"I think we can wait," Betty said. "We might need to have a cookie while we're waiting." She turned to Hannah. "What do you think?"

"It's a good plan!" Hannah exclaimed, excited to be in on the adventure, whatever it was.

Mist left the room, returning a few minutes later. She smiled at Betty and then took a seat near Hannah. "I found a solution to the problem," she announced.

"I knew you would," Betty said. "There was no doubt in my mind."

"What is it?" Hannah said, her voice excited.

Mist looked over each shoulder and then leaned toward Hannah. "I can have a flower girl if I can just find a girl around... let's see... six or seven years old."

"I'm seven!" Hannah said, jumping up and down,

"That's right!" Mist exclaimed. "*You* could be my flower girl! If you want to, that is."

"Yes, yes, yes!" Hannah stopped suddenly. "Oh. I need to ask my mom." She spun around and ran out of the room.

Betty looked at Mist and laughed. "And just what do you think Elaine will say?"

"Let me see..." Mist tapped her finger against her lips and then smiled. "I imagine she'll give Hannah the same answer she gave me a few minutes ago. She'll say yes."

TEN

Mist entered the front parlor, finding Violet and Rose admiring the Christmas tree, Burton reading a book on local history, and Elaine and both children working at a holiday craft table in the back of the room. Nat King Cole serenaded the room with images of chestnuts roasting on an open fire while indeed a fire—sans chestnuts—in the fireplace warmed the room. Clara and Andrew, relaxing on the couch, were deep in conversation with Michael.

"You two always take a midyear trip somewhere," Michael said. "Last year it was to Amsterdam, wasn't it?"

"Yes," Clara said. "That was wonderful. All those tulips! But you'll love where we went this year! You tell them, Andrew." She smiled as she accepted a cookie from Mist's offering.

"Hawaii!" Andrew announced.

"How lovely," Mist said. Taking a place next to Michael's chair, she rested her hand on his shoulder. "Which island? I've heard they're all unique."

"That's what we heard too. We had friends tell us to island hop," Clara said. "But we really wanted to relax, so we stayed on Maui the whole time, which was wonderful. We had the cutest little cottage by the beach. I adored it."

"We took day trips from there," Andrew said. "A highlight was driving to Hana. The hairpin turns were nerve-racking, but it was worth it for the gorgeous scenery."

"And the food!" Clara exclaimed. "I'd never tried ahi poke before, which we ordered at a little café in Lahaina. It was delicious."

"What is that, exactly?" Michael asked.

Andrew spoke up. "It's raw tuna with soy sauce, onion, and seasonings. I'd never had it either, but it's very traditional."

"And don't forget the shave ice," Clara said. "So refreshing!"

"Shouldn't that be *shaved* ice?" a new voice chimed in. All four turned to see the professor, ever the grammarian, enter the room and take a place on the end of the sofa, next to Clara and Andrew.

"Not in this case," Andrew said. "It's called *shave* ice there."

"You two should think about doing some traveling," Clara said, directing her comment to Mist and Michael. "As long as you're always here for Christmas, of course!" she added.

"There's no better place to be for Christmas than Timberton," the professor said. "But this is a good point about the travel. Michael, you'll have a good block of time off from teaching next summer. You and Mist should take a trip somewhere."

"We really should," Michael said, turning to Mist. "You know Betty could handle hotel guests for a couple of the summer weeks. Maisie would help her out, I'm sure. The question is: Where would you want to go?"

The notion of leaving Timberton for even a short while took Mist by surprise. Not that she didn't have favorite escapes around the area, whether for pleasure or work or both. She'd grown fond of several antique stores within an hour or two of the hotel, even struck up a friendship with one of the owners. On those trips they often closed up the shop and went next door for tea and conversation. She'd also made trips to Missoula and back frequently over the years to see Michael at the university. But to specifically go on a vacation was a new thought, oddly enough.

"An interesting question," Mist said finally. "I suppose there are many places that would be wonderful to see. Nothing touristy or crowded though. Someplace peaceful and serene, maybe with intriguing art and cuisine."

"You might mix the two," the professor suggested. "A city with great museums surrounded by small towns with local culture."

"Rome, perhaps," Andrew said.

"Or Paris," Violet said, joining the conversation. "Rose and I went there years ago and loved it."

Mist considered that. "It would be such a gift to see the Sistine Chapel. Or the collections in the Louvre."

"And combine those visits with trips into the countryside," Michael said. "Small villages, local cafés, vineyards."

"London, of course, would be brilliant," the professor said. "I have cousins there who could show you around. That is, if I'm not there to do it. I'm overdue for a trip back home."

"Japan could be fascinating," Andrew offered. "Or Thailand or…"

"Taos," Mist said, thinking out loud.

"Taos?" Michael repeated, intrigued. "New Mexico?"

"Yes," Mist said. "Culture and history and art. I've always thought it would be fascinating to go there. Or Sedona."

"Arizona…," Michael mused. "Not a bad idea. To see the red rocks."

Mist smiled. "And to feel the energy."

"Oh yes," Andrew said. "I've read about that. Vortexes, right?"

"Technically, the word is *vortices*," the professor asserted. "But I realize that's not the common usage."

"Hence the advantage of having you around," Andrew said. "We always learn something new when we see you."

"Glad to be of service." The professor took a mock bow.

"Did you always want to be an artist and chef?" Violet asked, somewhat out of the blue.

Mist tilted her head to one side. "Yes and no. I loved to draw and paint as far back as I can remember. But the interest in cooking came around when I worked at a beachside café in order to pay college tuition. It fascinated me to prepare and present food in order to please people. It became another form of art to me—different materials, different results, but art all the same."

"We're doing art projects," Hannah said, waving a collage of Christmas pictures in the air. One partially glued piece flew off and landed on Alex's head, causing a light quibble between the two siblings.

"And speaking of projects," Elaine said, "I told Millie I'd help at the library. I should get going. Burton, could you come supervise the craft table? It's getting a little wild over here."

"On my way," Burton said. He closed the book, began to tuck it under his arm, and then appeared to reconsider. Setting it on a bookshelf, he moved to the craft table and, somewhat shyly, started a collage of his own.

Taking this as a cue to move on to hotel tasks, Mist left the guests to the holiday music and various afternoon activities. She stopped by the kitchen, where she found Betty whipping up a new batch of glazed cinnamon nuts.

"Can barely keep the bowl full!" Betty exclaimed. "Makes you wonder if having children in the house makes a difference." She winked.

Mist laughed. "You do know the neighborhood kids are wise to that bowl, too, don't you?"

"Of course I know!" Betty said. "And I wouldn't have it any other way! We are getting low on walnuts, believe it or not."

"I have more over at the house," Mist said. "I'll go get some. I want to walk over anyway. Michael has told me it's off-limits tomorrow."

"I heard about that," Betty said, grinning. "It turns out he's a touch superstitious about seeing his bride on their wedding day."

"So I've been told." Mist smiled. "It'll be fine. I'll have plenty to keep me busy. I plan to help deliver the Christmas Joy baskets."

"Good." Betty grinned again. "Because you're not allowed in the front parlor tomorrow either. Maisie's orders."

"Am I allowed in the kitchen?" Mist said, her expression one of mock concern.

"Barely," Betty said. "Marge and I plan to have that all under control. Following your printed guidelines, of course. Thank you for spelling out the details of the Christmas Eve dinner."

"You're welcome. And thank you, all of you."

"It takes a village," Betty said.

Mist smiled. "Or a wonderful little mountain town."

TWELVE

A winter night was always a fitting time for a hot meal, which was why Mist had prepared two pasta casseroles with sun-dried tomatoes, mushrooms, and mozzarella cheese—one with Italian sausage, one without for those who preferred a meatless entrée. While the pasta dishes were baking, she tossed a mixed-green salad together with cranberries and walnuts and placed it in the refrigerator to keep chilled. Warm sourdough loaves boasting butter, garlic, and Parmesan cheese would accompany the meal. A simple lemon sorbet would follow for those who desired dessert. It was not a complicated meal, but it didn't need to be. Pasta, salad, bread, and sorbet would satisfy appetites and, as always, be an occasion for camaraderie. And that camaraderie, on this particular evening, would take place in more than one location.

"Your friendly mountain messenger service reporting for duty!" Clive's hearty voice accompanied his arrival through the kitchen's side door. He set a large canvas duffel bag on the center island, unzipped it, and waited for directions.

"I'm impressed!" Betty rewarded Clive with a kiss and then proceeded to pack the bag with take-out containers filled with pasta, salad, and bread. Knowing that lemon sorbet would be lemon soup if sent out with the other dishes, a selection of treats from the cookie exchange took the place of the frozen dessert. Mist added napkins, plates, and silverware.

"Will that be enough?" Clive asked as Betty zipped the bag closed.

"If nothing disappears on your way to the library, it will." Betty chuckled. "Let's see... Millie, Marge, Glenda, Sally, Maisie, Clayton... Who else is over there working on the baskets?" She looked to Mist for an answer.

"Elaine went over to help," Mist said. "And I heard a rumor that William Guthrie was going to be there too." Betty and Mist exchanged grins, causing Clive to look at both of them with a puzzled expression.

"I suspect that's because Sally is there," Betty whispered to Clive.

Clive let out a slow whistle. "Well, I'll be a muskrat's uncle! I'm sure slow to catch on to this." He shook his head. "Another one bites the dust!"

"Oh, so that's how you see it, do you?" Betty crossed her arms and tapped one foot while holding back a laugh.

"Of *course* not in our case, dear!" Clive crooned with an exaggerated tone. He gave Betty a hug and turned back for the duffel bag. "Ready?" Mist and Betty gestured to the door.

"I can take a hint, ladies, but stand forewarned. I'll be back!" Chuckling, Clive headed off to the library.

It didn't take long for Mist and Betty to put the rest of the food on the buffet. Hungry guests and townsfolk soon began to arrive, taking various places based on the number in their party and, even more so, anticipated conversations. Mist watched this with gratitude for the shared experiences within the group.

With Elaine helping over at the library, Hannah and Alex arrived with their father, taking seats at a large table. Seeing the boy from the library enter with his parents, Alex waved him over, and the two families sat together.

Clara and Andrew took seats with Violet and Rose, all relatively similar in age. They joked that they were the "senior table" though they allowed anyone to sit with them who could name a popular song from the 1950s or 60s. The criteria soon changed to include any song from before 2000 as more asked to join, and their table filled with others eager to reminisce about music from the past.

"I'm going with 'Hound Dog,'" Clive said as he returned from his deliveries and requested permission to join the table.

"I didn't take you for an Elvis fan," Clara said, reaching for her water glass.

"Why not? That guy had some smooth moves!" Clive did a little spin with some hip swings thrown in for good measure, which almost caused Clara to choke on her water.

"I'll stick with my lads from Liverpool," the professor said. "It's 'Eleanor Rigby' for me." He'd dressed for dinner, complete with red bow tie.

Betty joined the table with "My Way," clasping her hands over her heart as she named the tune.

"Ah, Frank Sinatra," Andrew said. "What a voice he had."

Even with a handful of other families and townsfolk stopping in for the meal, it was a small crowd overall with so many at the library. The café emptied earlier than usual as townsfolk headed home and hotel guests moved to the front parlor. Clara, Rose, and Violet settled in for conversation near the fireplace, which Clive had stoked after the meal. Andrew and the professor took places at a side table, the attraction there being a chessboard. Michael relaxed in his favorite chair with a book, as was his habit. And the Sadlers retired early, both their children being exhausted from the busy day.

That suited Mist and Betty well, as there was much to do to prepare for the next day. Betty convinced Mist—one might say she insisted—on giving her a list of kitchen tasks that she could do as prep work for the big dinner the following night. Mist, having a particular agenda for the evening, was easily convinced. She retrieved a pen and paper and made a list, urging Betty not to do more than she wanted to.

Mist made her way down the hallway behind the kitchen to the back room that had been a refuge for so many years, a place to create art, a place to sleep, a place to enjoy solitude even when the hotel itself was busy. And a place where, once a year, she would gather small canvases, one for each visiting guest, and create a miniature painting to accompany them home after the holidays. For all that she believed in memories being the most precious gift of all, she also knew something tangible could evoke memories much like a piece of music or a favorite food.

Traditionally, Mist would complete these small gifts on Christmas Eve, late at night, after guests had retired for the evening. However, this year necessitated a different timetable, and she had planned on this evening to create the gifts. And so she gathered the canvases and set them into a frame that Clive had made her long ago to hold multiples of the four-by-four-inch squares. Knowing already what the images would be, she chose paint colors to reflect the holidays: a deep red, hunter green, soft gold, and others—and began to paint.

A sweet pleasure of working late at night was the stillness that allowed her mind to wander and create. So it was a surprise when a noise outside caught her attention. Curious more than concerned, she set her brush down and moved to her window, which looked out over the back property. Expecting something blown by the wind or even wildlife—not uncommon in the small mountain town—passing through, she was surprised to see a person on the sloping portion of the land that led to the door that Hollister used to come and go from his room downstairs. In fact, the jacket on the person looked very much like the one Hollister wore, as did the hat on his head. But what was he doing outside this time of night? And then she saw something that made her gasp. Could it be?

Grabbing a shawl from a hook on her wall, she slipped on her boots and stepped out into the hallway. Moving downstairs, she prepared to tap on Hollister's door but found it slightly ajar, enough that she gave herself permission to step inside, feeling a rush of cold air as she did. And there she found Hollister kneeling down just outside his open back door, one hand gently resting on a light brown dog's head, the other holding a strip of bacon.

An unexpected warmth filled her heart at the sight of the sweet dog and even sweeter man. Their facial expressions, human and canine, said the exact same thing: each had found a best friend.

Mist crossed the floor and crouched down in the back doorway. An initial worried look on Hollister's face turned to relief when Mist gestured for him to bring the dog into the room. Once inside, Mist closed the door and patted the foot of Hollister's bed. The dog jumped onto the bedspread and curled up. She gave the dog a gentle caress and then gave Hollister a hug to confirm her approval.

Leaving the two to enjoy their home together, she returned to her room and settled back at her easel. And as she lost herself in painting, she smiled at the lingering image of Hollister's expression: that of sheer joy.

THIRTEEN

As was traditional for the morning of Christmas Eve, breakfast was casual and limited to hotel guests. All the intricacies and details of meal preparation and presentation would go into the feast to be served that evening.

Awake long before dawn, Mist lay in bed, eyes open, heart beating with anticipation of a day that would match no other in her life. She marveled at the idea of holiday festivities, friendship, and love all intersecting for a moment in time, a day in time. A day she had looked forward to for a year. A day she was certain to remember forever.

The kitchen was quiet and dark when she entered. She knew Betty would still be sleeping, and the guests wouldn't begin to appear until she put the coffee out an hour later. Pulling a tapered candle from a kitchen drawer, she placed it in a pewter candle holder and set it in the middle of the kitchen island. She struck a match, noting the *whoosh* as it caught fire along with the whisper as she blew it out. In the silence of the morning, each sound seemed amplified, more intense than usual.

In the soft glow of candlelight, Mist gently combined ingredients that would enter the oven as lovingly mixed batter and exit in due time as either apple-cinnamon muffins, ready to join bowls of mixed berries, granola, and yogurt on the breakfast buffet, or sweet lemon cake for later that evening. The muffins and other breakfast sides would be just enough to hold the guests over until the extravagant meal later on. A midafternoon presentation of cheese and crackers would take care of any truly eager appetites. And Betty's glazed cinnamon nuts always stood ready for a needed snack.

Mist filled the muffin pans and slid them in the oven. Mixing the lemon cake batter next, she set it aside to go into the oven once the muffins came out. As a hint of apples and cinnamon began to float through the air, she set up the beverage area in the front lobby, knowing guests would soon be looking for their first cup of coffee or tea. Hot chocolate would also be available all day as well as a heated pot of hot cider. Glass canning jars holding peppermint and cinnamon sticks would accompany the beverages throughout the day in case anyone's hot chocolate or cider needed sprucing up.

Returning to the kitchen, she followed an impulse and put a cast-iron frying pan on the stovetop, which soon had sizzling strips of bacon adding to the aroma of the baked goods.

"I thought you were only going to serve muffins and berries this morning," Betty said, spying the bacon cooking as she entered the kitchen in a bathrobe with a reindeer print. Her words were followed by a large yawn as she took a mug from a cabinet and poured herself coffee from the small kitchen coffee maker.

Mist smiled as she watched Betty take a seat at the kitchen island. "I felt a sudden inspiration."

"Really." Betty blew across the top of her coffee and then took a sip. "You're not making very much," she observed, counting the number of strips in the pan.

"We won't need much," Mist replied. "This is for a special guest. You might even say a new employee who can help with leftovers." Mist's expression took on an impish grin as she flipped the bacon over. She was unabashedly pleased with herself for having a secret that no one else knew. Except Hollister, of course.

Betty chuckled. "I'm not even going to ask. You'll tell me when you're ready. It's your special day. Oh, speaking of which, you're not allowed in the front parlor today. Maisie's orders."

"In that case, I'll just have to find other things to do," Mist quipped. "There must be something going on today that I can find to keep busy." She lifted the bacon out of the pan with a spatula and, to Betty's surprise, placed it in a reusable food container and closed the lid.

This time Betty laughed outright. "Like serving breakfast, delivering baskets to the community, preparing a dinner feast, and getting married?"

"Now that you put it that way, it does sound like a busy day." Mist set the bacon container aside and checked the oven. Deciding the muffins were ready, she pulled them out and slid the lemon cake in. She closed the oven, set a timer, and removed the muffins from the pans, setting them aside on wire racks. Once cool, she placed them in a fabric-lined basket and added them to the buffet with whipped butter and honey.

Hotel guests wandered in at their leisure, having been told this was a light, casual breakfast buffet that they could come to whenever they wanted. Despite the whirlwind of activity taking place, this was still vacation for them, a time to relax during the holidays, a break from their busier lives.

Still, the excitement in the air could not be ignored. As often happened, hotel guests and townsfolk had become involved in each other's lives even in the short amount of time since many had met. Clara and Rose bundled up in jackets, mittens, and hats and went for a morning walk together. Elaine grabbed a muffin to go and went to the library, having told Millie she'd love to help with the Christmas Joy basket delivery. Clayton arrived with Maisie to help deliver an oversized floral structure to the now "off-limits to Mist" front parlor before heading to the library. Betty raved about it when she entered the kitchen, reminding Mist quickly that she was forbidden to go look.

The professor had tea in the café with Burton—who finally seemed to be relaxing into the flow of things—and then stepped into the parlor to help arrange furniture for the late-evening event. One by one, apple-cinnamon muffins headed off in all directions as people moved on to whatever activity they had planned.

At last, Mist and Betty sat at the kitchen island, breakfast dishes put away, and went over a list of tasks for the Christmas Eve dinner. Although Mist had planned the meal and done as much advance work as possible, she had wisely agreed to let Betty and Clara help that afternoon and evening to make sure the Christmas Eve dinner proceeded without a hitch.

"I started putting the serving dishes and utensils on the buffet." Betty looked down a list of platters and bowls to be used that evening. "I'm short two trays, I think."

"Those will be inside one of the lower cabinets in the buffet," Mist said. "Try the middle door."

Betty made a trip into the café and returned quickly with two trays under her arm. "You should see how enthralled Hannah is, sorting pieces of lace, yarn, and ribbon into small piles out there on a café table. Bringing out that tub of sewing scraps was a clever idea."

"I knew she'd want something to do after breakfast," Mist said, walking over to join Betty. She watched the child hold up a string of gold sequins, deciding which pile to add it to. "She's going to help deliver the Christmas Joy baskets, but she needed an activity to fill the time before meeting at the library. She's quite intriguing."

"Much the way I imagine you were so many years ago," Betty said as she and Mist both moved back into the kitchen. "Bright in spirit, full of imagination, eager to embrace life."

"I suppose I was a bit like that," Mist admitted, thinking back to her childhood. "I was always curious about life. Reality and imagination tended to flow together. I'm not sure I knew where one ended and the other began."

Betty chuckled. "And you do now?"

"Are they not intertwined?" Mist mused.

"I suppose they are," Betty said. "You've taught us that, you know. You've taught us all so much since you came to Timberton."

Mist smiled. "You give me too much credit. We learn what we're ready to learn. We absorb it. I've learned from you and Clive, from the community here in Timberton. I didn't know it at the time, but moving here was a tremendous gift in my life."

"Sort of like it was supposed to happen all along?" Betty mused.

"Yes." Mist smiled. "It was meant to be."

FOURTEEN

The library was a flurry of activity when Mist arrived. Festive baskets decked out with ribbons and tiny bells graced every library table, cart, and counter in the building. Town vendors wandered from one group of baskets to the next, checking the contents and shuffling items here and there to make sure each had a variety of gifts. The baskets—remarkably, two hundred of them—were not identical in what they held, but all offered an assortment of items designed to bring joy to its recipient home. One household might find flowers, homemade cookies, and scented candles. Another could receive a whimsical ornament, maple-nut fudge, and cocoa packets. All would find a decorated sheet with a Christmas message prepared by local children.

"I can't even believe you're here, considering how much you have going on today," Millie exclaimed upon seeing Mist watching the commotion. "Do you mind if I call you a crazy person?"

"You may call me anything you'd like, Millie," Mist replied with a grin.

"Just don't call her late for dinner," Clive quipped from a nearby table where he and Clayton, both wearing Santa hats, were placing baskets into boxes to carry. Seeing both women roll their eyes at the overused phrase, he added, "What? Someone had to say it! That's the beauty of clichés!"

"Beauty is in the eye of the beholder," Clayton said. "But in this case, since Mist feeds most of us, *definitely* do not call her late for dinner!"

Millie laughed. "You two make quite the comedy team. Let's get those baskets loaded up."

"I saw the fire truck out in front, Clayton," Mist said. "It's such a wonderful idea to deliver the baskets with it. Children of all ages will be delighted."

"I admit it's an odd-looking sleigh, but at least it's red," Clayton said.

"With a fancy Christmas wreath on the bumper," Maisie added as she approached, Clay Jr. by her side.

Clayton winked. "The advantage of marrying a florist!"

Mist bent down and smiled at Clay Jr. "I'm going to see you later for something special, right?"

The small boy nodded his head. "I'm gonna be your helper."

"His outfit is all ready," Maisie said. "He's very excited about his role as ring bearer."

"You'll be a great helper!" Mist said.

"I will be!" Clay Jr. repeated with enthusiasm. "I know how to stand still now!"

"We've been practicing," Maisie whispered.

Mist laughed, appreciating the effort, though it didn't matter to her if the child exhibited his usual energy, which was likely to involve no shortage of hopping around. The wedding was intended to be a short, sweet, cheerful occasion without formality. A child's enthusiasm could only add a sense of lightness to the event.

Box by box, Clayton and his crew, along with Clive, carried the baskets out to the fire truck, tucking them into multiple sections wherever they could share space with fire-fighting equipment. Due to the clear weather, some were able to be loaded on top of the truck. Clayton's fire chief vehicle would follow the fire truck, which his crew members would drive. This allowed whatever baskets didn't fit in and on the truck itself to be delivered on the same round as the others.

"Do I get to ride along?" Clay Jr. asked, shifting his weight from one foot to the other.

"How often do you get to ride in that fire truck?" Maisie asked with a hint of a smile.

"Um… all the time," the young boy answered.

"That's right. So maybe just for today we can let someone else ride up front. Like someone who is having a special day today." She looked at Mist. "Do you have time? It should take about an hour."

Mist thought this over. She'd intended to return to the hotel as soon as the deliveries started. But spending an hour out in the community, dropping off gifts, sounded appealing, and suddenly she knew she didn't want to pass up the opportunity. "Why not? Are you going?"

Maisie shook her head. "I have a few things to do to get ready for some kind of special event tonight. Can't remember what it is…" She scratched her head as if trying to remember.

"Everyone is a comedian today." Mist laughed as she exited the library and headed to the bright red truck in the parking lot, a festive sight with ribboned baskets peeking out of compartments and gracing the top of the vehicle.

"Aha! A passenger of honor!" Clayton moved to the right side of the fire truck and helped Mist climb into the seat, which involved several steps and a tight hold on a hand grip. Once seated, the crew took their seats and the deliveries began.

Looking at the town from the height of her seat, Mist wondered if she'd ever been able to view Timberton from a similar vantage point. From what she could recall, she hadn't. She'd often walked the streets, preferring to run errands on foot when possible. And she'd driven in and out of town at a normal level of vision for a car. But to see the shops and houses from the height she was at now was unique, even thrilling, as if she were seeing the town she loved for the first time.

The first residential area started just beyond Clive's gallery. Clayton and his crew brought the vehicles to a stop halfway down the block. Millie, Marge, and Glenda, who had ridden along with Clayton, each took a basket from the back of his car. Clayton and his crew pulled deliveries from the fire truck, starting with those on the roof. And Mist, determined to soak in every ounce of the experience, slid down from her seat—which gave her the unexpected thrill of a schoolgirl on a slide—and chose a basket from a side compartment. Spreading out, they approached each house, placing a basket at the front door.

From the first area, they moved to another, and then another, until all the baskets had been distributed. They gathered back at the library and briefly shared their experiences.

Many families had opened their doors before the baskets made it up their walkways, having heard the fire truck pull up. Though the Community Joy Project had never been a secret, the delighted expressions of surprise that greeted the deliveries made it seem like it was so. One family with young children had opened their door amidst squeals of excitement. A middle-aged man who was known to generally be gruff had cracked a smile for the first time anyone could remember. And an elderly lady who lived alone had reacted with tears in her eyes as she accepted the gift. Mist had pulled her into her arms and held her as she cried. "Tears of joy," the woman had whispered, which Mist accepted as almost true, knowing memories came in all colors: some bright, some blue.

FIFTEEN

Mist found Betty and Marge in the kitchen, just as she expected. To her delight, the two had made big strides in preparing for the dinner that evening. Trays of maple-mustard carrots stood ready to go into the oven. Pineapple rings lined a roasting pan, waiting for two large hams to be added with a brown-sugar-honey glaze. Another pan, this one for herb-crusted prime rib, sat beside it. Portobello mushrooms and quinoa were measured and waiting to be made into a risotto closer to the dinner hour. And the ingredients for a crisp apple salad were set aside in the refrigerator, ready to be mixed together with a dijon vinaigrette just before being served.

Marge was just finishing a pecan crumble to add to a sweet potato casserole. Notes in Betty's handwriting adorned bowls and pans, indicating dishes that were oven-ready or needing additional ingredients. Betty had just started folding a stack of linen napkins.

"I knew you two were the right ones for the job," Mist said, pleased to see everything coming together. "You both look so organized, which doesn't surprise me at all."

"I made the brioche rolls over at the shop," Marge said. "They're rising now. I'll bring them over once they're baked. They'll just need to be reheated before serving."

"That will be fine," Mist said. "The ham will need to rest when it comes out of the oven. It will be just the right amount of time to heat the rolls. The other hot dishes will be in the other oven." A feeling of gratitude, not for the first time, washed over her, thinking about the second oven Clive had installed in the kitchen after the Moonglow Café moved into the hotel.

"How did it go with the basket deliveries?" Betty asked. "I'll bet people loved them."

"They were thrilled. It was wonderful seeing the reactions. There were many happy faces, squeals of delight from children, and even tears of gratitude."

Mist picked up a copy of the printed dinner plan she'd left on the counter and ran a finger down the page, reconfirming details: oven temperatures, starting times for different dishes, and garnishes that needed to be added at the last minute. She was pleased, even a little charmed, at seeing check marks and margin notes that Betty and Marge had made while working.

Setting the paper aside, she pulled a full apron off a wall hook and slipped the upper strap over her head. The holly print on the fabric complemented the hunter-green rayon skirt she'd chosen to wear that day. It was one of several holiday aprons she and Betty had found at Second Hand Sally's.

"You're going to *work*?" Betty said as she and Marge exchanged looks.

Mist glanced around while tying the apron. "I don't see any work. I see the makings of a culinary feast, of a chance to spend time with two wonderful friends, of a lovely way to spend a holiday afternoon."

"But you must have things to do," Marge said.

Mist pulled a bowl of fresh cranberries and sliced pears out of the refrigerator. "And just what would those things be?"

"Getting ready for tonight?" Betty and Marge spoke at the same time.

Mist couldn't help but smile at the concerned looks on Betty's and Marge's faces. It's possible someone else would be running around, attending to last-minute details for the wedding that evening. Instead, she planned to make cranberry-pear sauce to go with lemon cake baked that morning for the evening's dessert.

"Who's officiating?" Marge asked. "I keep meaning to ask."

Betty chuckled. "She won't tell us."

Marge looked at Mist. "Seriously?"

"It's a surprise," Mist said, grinning. "We lost the person we'd arranged a few weeks ago. Fortunately, someone perfect offered to get certified for it."

"It must be Clive," Marge said.

Betty shook her head. "He would have told me… I think… wouldn't he?"

"I would think so," Marge said.

Betty folded another linen napkin and set it aside. "Maybe it's Wild Bill. Now *that* would be a hoot!"

"It certainly would be!" Marge turned back to Mist. "So you really feel everything is ready? What about your dress?"

"Hanging upstairs in a dressing room."

"Your hair?"

"Glenda is going to help me with it after dinner."

Betty and Marge began to alternate questions.

"What about something old?"

"New?"

"Borrowed?"

"Blue?"

Mist laughed. "Maisie says she has that covered."

"Oh!" Marge exclaimed suddenly. "Speaking of having things covered, I'd better go check on those rolls." She washed the remnants of pecan crumble off her hands, grabbed her jacket, and left by way of the side door.

"Alex seems to have made a friend here." Betty nodded toward the kitchen window, and Mist walked over to take a look. Alex and the boy from the library were engaged in a fast-paced snowball fight. Equal measures of shouting and laughter soared through the air along with the tightly packed balls of snow.

"I'm pleased to see that," Mist said. "Elaine mentioned that he's been withdrawn since his best friend moved away recently."

"It's a shame they don't live closer together," Betty mused. "They seem to get along well."

"True," Mist replied. "But I don't think distance is important in this case. It's the lesson that matters.

Alex has learned it's possible to make new friends. It may not take long for him to form a new friendship once he's home."

"Good point," Betty said. "He certainly seems much happier now than when he first arrived. In fact, so does Rose. Have you noticed? Maybe she's made a new friend too. She and Clara have been spending time together."

Mist moved back to the cranberries and pears, prepared to add sugar and spices before putting them on the stove to cook. "Her time with Clara has been healing. She's seen the life Clara has built after losing her husband years ago. That gives her hope that she can do the same."

"We all need hope," Betty mused. "Christmas seems to kindle that around here. It inspires us."

Mist smiled, thinking about Betty's statement. That had always been her goal, not only for the holidays but throughout the year. Yet Christmas did seem to bring with it an extra touch of inspiration amidst holiday decorations, music, treats, and simply time spent together.

"It does," Mist said as she set the cranberries and pears on the stove in a saucepan. She then added sugar, water, and a splash of orange juice before sprinkling cinnamon and ginger on top. She adjusted the burner to the appropriate level and turned back to Betty. "I feel there's a sort of magic to Christmas here in Timberton. I've always felt that."

"I feel that too." Betty finished folding the last napkin and set it aside with the others, ready for the tables in the café. "I've especially felt it since you arrived, dear Mist."

Mist replied softly, "You're so kind, Betty. You know as well as I do that the credit belongs to everyone. It's contagious, you know. Hope. We pass it to each other and beyond."

"I suppose you're right, now that I think about it."

Mist crossed the room, gave Betty a hug, and before returning to the stove, whispered in her ear, "Of course I'm right."

SIXTEEN

Christmas Eve Dinner Menu

Honey-glazed ham with pineapple
Herb-crusted prime rib
Crisp apple salad with dijon vinaigrette
Portobello mushroom quinoa risotto
Sweet potato casserole with pecan crumble
Maple-mustard roasted carrots with
ginger-cashew cream
Herbed brioche dinner rolls
Lemon cake with cranberry-pear sauce

O f all the traditions Mist held dear when it came to the holidays at the hotel, some felt especially close to her heart. It was a small but important one that she embraced this evening: the quiet time she always spent alone in the Moonglow Café before the Christmas Eve dinner guests arrived. This precious time brought her a sense of peace.

She moved through the room quietly, stopping at each table, straightening a centerpiece here, adjusting a crystal water glass there. Just the motion of touching each table in some way made her feel closer to the guests who would soon come together to share the meal. Perhaps, she thought, it would even make the guests feel closer to her in some unexplainable way. She lit small votive candles along the buffet, switched on tiny white lights that hung in scalloped fashion from the ceiling, and started soft Christmas instrumental music.

This being a special night in many ways, she had taken extra care in dressing for the dinner hour, creating an outfit that felt like a step toward the enchanting change of clothing that would occur later in the evening. For now, for the next few hours, she would wear a vintage dress in a muted red hue, just bright enough to add to the holiday spirit without being too loud. She'd wrapped an ivory shawl around her waist, letting it float above the hemline, which fell midcalf above a pair of ivory flats. A single string of pearls graced her neckline, a simple style that offered a touch of sophistication, matched with pearl earrings. An off-white lace headband held her hair back from her face yet allowed it to fall freely around her shoulders, ready for Glenda to style it—something *simple*, Mist had urged—after dinner.

In a move that struck Mist as sweet though surprising, Michael had decided to skip dinner, just as he'd opted out of helping with the basket deliveries. The reason for this, he had explained, was the tradition of the groom not seeing the bride on their wedding day. Mist's reaction to this had been both surprised and charmed. She viewed superstition as being a somewhat ethereal mix of fate and magic, an attempt by people to understand cause and effect where there often wasn't a relationship between the two.

She moved to the doorway and prepared to open it to the guests and townsfolk waiting outside. Before doing so, she took one last look around the café and let the peaceful yet festive scene settle into her heart, warming it with the knowledge that others would enjoy the same surroundings. Pleased, she opened the doors and stood back to greet people.

Clara and Andrew entered first, accompanied by Violet and Rose. All four boasted attire in holiday colors: a red dress here, a green vest there, and accessories—snowflake earrings, silver bangles, a blinking necklace of tiny lights, and gold cuff links— adding a touch of Christmas to their outfits. They took seats together at their self-appointed "senior table" and began to chat while waiting for others to arrive.

Clive, having closed the gallery in plenty of time to dress for dinner, sauntered in decked out in dress slacks, a collared shirt, and a cable-knit sweater. He grinned and pumped his thumb over his shoulder. Seconds later, Wild Bill followed, and—to no one's surprise now—he was not alone. Sally's hand rested lightly in the crook of his arm. No doubt remained about their new status as a couple. Both radiated happiness as they entered the room.

The Sadlers arrived together, parents and children dressed casually but nicely for the occasion. Mist grinned at the sight of reindeer antlers on both Elaine's and Burton's heads, an indication that the family had found a comfortable lightness during their visit.

Missing from the mix, the professor had chosen to stay with Michael so he wouldn't have to eat alone. Knowing this in advance, Mist had sent dinner fare down to the new residence, where they could enjoy the same meal as the others.

Table by table, the café filled. Tiny lights flickered above, and music floated from one favorite melody to the next as Bing Crosby, Frank Sinatra, and Perry Como serenaded the joyful crowd. Conversation flowed freely as guests and townsfolk enjoyed the sumptuous buffet offerings.

"Delicious as always!" Clive exclaimed, having just filled his plate with second servings. This started a chorus of similar compliments around the room.

"The glazed ham is fabulous!"

"Best sweet potatoes I've ever had!"

"Those brioche rolls are perfection with butter!"

"I simply must get that risotto recipe!"

Mist graciously accepted the praise, noting that Betty and Marge deserved much of the credit. The meal had been a team effort, one she was grateful for.

As she moved from table to table, refilling water glasses and making sure everyone felt welcome, a slight movement drew her attention toward the lobby. To her surprise, Hollister stood just outside the door to the café. Thrilled to see him there—he rarely entered the common areas of the hotel—she caught his eye and smiled, earning a smile in return. Could it be, after all these years, that he might join them?

She looked around for an empty chair, spotting two at the table where Clive sat along with Betty, who had finally been convinced to rest. Glancing from the empty seats to Hollister and back in order to form a nonverbal suggestion, she walked to the café door and stepped out, turning to face into the café beside Hollister. Slipping her hand inside his arm just as Sally had when she arrived with Wild Bill, she waited.

Of all the times Mist had felt something special was about to take place inside the Timberton Hotel, this fell high on the list. This gentle person, previously homeless and living below the railroad trestle, had only moved into the back hotel room after several years of encouragement. He'd only entered the main hotel a handful of times, those occasions only brief glances from a distance. Now he stood at the door to the Moonglow Café for the most anticipated event of the season. He had taken many small steps over the years. This would be a large one.

Mist felt the movement as soon as it happened, the forward motion of his first step. She squeezed his arm as a sign of encouragement, and together they walked toward Clive and Betty's table, where they settled into the open chairs. Betty reached over and squeezed Hollister's hand, and Clive nodded, both letting him know they were pleased to see him join in.

A trip to the buffet table allowed Hollister to fill his plate with glazed ham, maple-mustard roasted carrots, sweet potato with pecan crumble, and much more. Mist chose only a light serving of crisp apple salad with spicy maple vinaigrette, just something to accompany him along the buffet. After they returned to the table and took their seats, Mist became aware of movement by her feet as Hollister discreetly reached below the table with a carrot slice. Which was when, to her delight, she realized she had welcomed not one but two new guests to the Christmas Eve dinner.

Mist excused herself, a sudden thought occurring to her. She found a scratch paper and pen in the kitchen and returned to the table. Writing the word *name* and a question mark at the top of the sheet, she wrote out a list of possible names for the dog and slid the paper over to Hollister. He picked it up, looked over the choices, and then turned it over, finding a grocery list on the back. He smiled, circled a word, and handed it back to Mist, who covered her mouth to keep from laughing out loud. She took the pen and wrote *okay!* next to the word he'd circled. And from that moment on, the new hotel resident would be called, appropriately, Bacon.

Assured that Hollister was in good company, Mist checked the buffet to see what refills were needed and retreated to the kitchen, where she found Maisie waiting at the kitchen island, plates of lemon cake and cranberry-pear sauce ready to serve.

"This is an amazing night in many ways," Maisie said.

"Yes, it is." Mist attempted to say more but was struck with more sentiment than she could put into words. She reached for a dessert plate but stopped when she felt a hand on her arm. She turned to see Betty.

"I believe you get the next few hours to yourself. That has been the plan." Betty's tone was kind but determined.

"And still *is* the plan," Maisie added. "The dinner is going smoothly, as always. Betty and Marge are going to serve dessert when the guests are ready."

"And there's an army of volunteers offering to help clean up," Betty said.

Maisie moved around the counter, took hold of Mist's hand, and smiled. "Let's go."

Mist looked back and forth between Betty and Maisie. Betty made a "shooing" gesture with her hands. Maisie followed this with raised eyebrows and a shrug of the shoulders. Finally, Mist let out a sigh of heartfelt gratitude for the kindness of friends.

"Okay," she said. "Let's go."

SEVENTEEN

The rooms on the second floor of the hotel all served as guest accommodations with the exception of one, which stored the few pieces of furniture not currently in use—an Eastlake dresser, several oak chairs, and a tall walnut wardrobe—as well as miscellaneous supplies that would otherwise have to be transported up and down the stairs daily. It had the potential to be used for overnight guests if needed, though it would require advance planning as the storage and supplies would need to be moved out, and a few minor repairs were due. But the room was spacious, so it served as a perfect spot for a pre-wedding dressing room.

Lively conversation dotted with bursts of laughter trailed from below as Mist and Maisie climbed the staircase to the second floor. As strange as it felt to leave the traditional dinner before it ended, Mist knew the event was in good hands. Betty and Marge had gone above and beyond to make everything perfect.

"Thank you, Maisie," Mist said as they reached the landing. "You've done so much to help. You and so many others."

"It's nothing compared to everything you do for all of us," Maisie said. "And that's every day, I might add. Not just on one special day like this."

"We all help each other, as it should be."

Mist followed Maisie to the spare room, puzzled when Maisie stopped and tapped on the door. A few seconds passed, and then Maisie opened the door, stepped aside, and gestured for Mist to enter. When she did, her eyes grew wide.

The transformation of the room took her breath away. Sweet clusters of white tulips, blue delphinium, and assorted winter greenery graced the tops of stored furniture. Light instrumental music flowed from corner speakers, and champagne flutes rested on a silver tray set near the walnut wardrobe, where Mist's wedding dress hung gracefully from a satin hanger.

"This is amazing!" Mist exclaimed, looking up into soft light cascading down from an old crystal chandelier, original to the hotel. "That hasn't worked in years!"

"Clive fixed it for this occasion," Maisie said. "We wanted you to have a special room to prepare for the wedding."

"Any room would be special with you in it." Mist directed her statement not only to Maisie but to Clara, who'd been waiting in the room already, and Betty, who'd just entered.

Maisie stepped to the table with the champagne flutes and lifted a bottle from an ice bucket as Glenda, Marge, Sally, and Millie also filed into the room. She looked at Mist and grinned. "Consider this an extremely delicate version of a bachelorette party. You have two hours before the ceremony. We're stealing thirty minutes of it to celebrate."

Mist looked around the room as a thought occurred to her. "If you're all here, who's serving dessert downstairs?" She directed her question to Betty and Marge, the two of them being the ones who had said they would be delivering the servings of lemon cake with cranberry-pear sauce.

"Will you worry if we say we left Clive and Clayton in charge?" Betty grinned.

"It's a definite possibility," Mist said, eliciting laughter all around. "But I suspect all will survive the challenge."

"Even Clive and Clayton," Maisie quipped as she popped the cork from the champagne bottle. Amidst more laughter, she poured the bubbly into the flutes and passed them around.

"I'd like to propose a toast," Maisie said, lifting her glass in the air. "To the person who gives us so much happiness. We wish you the most happiness of all."

Flutes clinked against each other as all joined in, and light conversation followed, much interspersed with laughter. Mist moved around the small room, breathing in the scents of each cluster of flowers, swaying to the music, and admiring the shimmer of light coming from the chandelier's crystals. She took only a few sips of champagne, wanting to keep a clear head for the important evening. Eventually, at Glenda's suggestion, she set her flute down and took a seat in front of a low dresser with an exquisite framed mirror.

"I know you want something simple," Glenda said. Standing behind Mist, she eased the lace headband off and ran her fingers through her hair. "Can you tell me what you have in mind?"

"Probably not a beehive." Clara grinned, and her statement was soon followed by others.

"Or a pompadour," Betty said, shaking her head.

"Definitely no sausage curls," Millie offered.

"I'd avoid a mullet," Maisie said. "Although that could be interesting with some color…" Her voice trailed off as laughter took over.

Mist relaxed against the back of the chair, entertained by the lighthearted discussion. Indeed, she wanted none of those styles. She closed her eyes, envisioned a finished look, and then spoke. "Windswept."

"Windswept," Glenda repeated.

"Yes," Mist said. "As if a gust of wind comes through and tosses everything in the air. Then it lands where it wants, some up, some down, with a few flowers scattered in the midst."

"We can do that! Windswept it is!" One part at a time, Glenda brushed out Mist's hair, letting most of it fall free while securing wispy sections at varying heights with hairpins. Maisie stood alongside, adding delicate flowers whenever Glenda indicated a spot was ready for one. In the end, all stood back and marveled at the sweet yet elegant style. Glenda had managed to capture the intended look.

Mist, thrilled with the finished style, stood and embraced Glenda. "It's perfect," she whispered.

"And it will look perfect with your dress," Maisie said, tapping her wristwatch to hint that time was passing.

"I think it's time we leave you and Maisie to attend to the final details," Betty said. "I'd better make sure Clive and Clayton didn't veer off task."

"Good idea," Mist said. She thanked each treasured friend for the impromptu party as the group departed, leaving only Maisie behind, who then moved to the walnut wardrobe.

"What do you say we trade that beautiful dress you wore to dinner for the beautiful one here?" Maisie gently removed the wedding dress from the hanger and waited while Mist slipped out of her dinner dress and stepped into the one she would wear for the ceremony. Maisie hung the dinner dress in the wardrobe and then attended to a long row of buttons that graced the back of Mist's dress. When finished, she stepped back and gave Mist a nod of approval.

"You're smiling," Mist noted as she stepped into satin flats that she'd decorated with beads to match the dress.

"Because you look like a princess bride from another galaxy, Mist, truly." Maisie wiped a tear from her eye. "I can't wait to see Michael's face when he sees you."

Mist smiled at the thought.

"You just need a few last touches," Maisie said, opening a wooden box on the dresser. She lifted out a lace handkerchief. "Something old. It's from Second Hand Sally's. She wanted you to have it."

"It's beautiful," Mist said. She admired an embroidered design of two doves and then slipped the handkerchief inside a dress sleeve.

Maisie reached back into the box and brought out a pair of dangling silver earrings with inlaid beads that matched the wedding dress. "I suppose I don't need to tell you this is something new, since you designed them."

"I suppose not." Mist laughed. "Clive did a wonderful job on these, didn't he?"

"They're beautiful," Maisie said. "As is this, which is something borrowed from Betty." She pinned a heart-shaped brooch near the neckline of Mist's dress.

"I love it."

"And then we have this…" Maisie plucked a tiny blue flower from an arrangement and added it to those already in Mist's hair.

"Perfect."

"One more thing," Maisie said, reaching into the box, lifting out a coin, which she handed to Mist.

"Dare I ask?"

"A sixpence for your shoe," Maisie explained. "An actual sixpence, which they don't make anymore, but the professor had one, so here you go."

Mist lifted one foot out of its satin flat and dropped the sixpence in. Stepping back into the shoe, she looked at Maisie. "Never let it be said that I went against the professor's wishes."

Maisie smiled, and the two embraced. "And now I think you're ready."

"Yes," Mist said. "I believe I am."

EIGHTEEN

Mist stood in the hotel entryway, the doors to the front parlor closed. Maisie stood to the side, helping Hannah and Clay Jr. stay in place, each holding the item of their assigned role: a single flower bouquet in lieu of petals for Hannah, a velvet pillow with two rings tied onto it with satin ribbons for Clay Jr.

Soft strains of Handel's "Air" from the Water Music suite flowed from beyond the closed doors. This delighted Mist, as she had wanted gentle music playing while guests mingled before the wedding, music that would not change when she entered other than to grow slightly louder in volume.

Maisie and Mist exchanged smiles, an unspoken sign that it was time to open the doors, which Maisie did. With a gentle nudge, Hannah and Clay Jr. started into the room. Hannah, in a sweet moment, took young Clay's hand. At first he pulled away, but he then looked at her with a sort of awe and accepted the gesture.

Mist stepped into the doorway behind the children, and the scene before her almost took her breath away.

An archway of white orchids, evergreen boughs, and shimmering silver ribbons framed the window of the front parlor. Tiny lights sparkled from within the foliage, adding an otherworldly effect. She understood why Betty had marveled when Maisie and Clayton had delivered it earlier in the day. It was by far the most elaborate floral design she'd ever seen, worthy of a glossy magazine showcasing a fairy-tale wedding.

The Christmas tree had been carefully moved to the corner of the room, a tight squeeze that caused the branches to caress the walls but enough of a change to center the exquisite arch in such a way as to be seen perfectly from both inside and outside the picture window.

And there, between the orchids and the evergreen branches, Michael waited, and everything else in the room seemed to disappear. There was only Michael, steadfast and confident, giving her a reassuring nod.

As the music grew louder, Mist moved forward one slow step at a time. In the intimate setting of the front parlor, it was only a short journey. Yet it felt as if she'd traveled from one world to the next. She soon stood next to Michael, and the two faced the professor, a very dignified-looking officiant in a tweed suit jacket and red—it was the holidays, after all—bow tie. In this attire, complete with wire-rimmed glasses and perfect posture, it was clear he commanded respect during the lectures he gave at the university.

The music faded away, and the professor spoke.

"Beloved friends, we gather here to celebrate Mist and Michael's love and commitment to each other. After watching their relationship blossom over the course of eight years, I can honestly say…" He pushed his glasses up on his nose. "…that it's about time."

A light wave of laughter floated through the room. As quiet settled in, he continued.

"I believe you have some vows, short though they may be." The professor looked from Michael to Mist and then back to Michael, who took Mist's hands in his.

"Mist, I've never met anyone quite like you, and I thank the universe, as you would say, for bringing you into my world. I'm honored to have the chance to spend my life with you."

The professor nodded his approval and turned to Mist.

"Michael, we are all surrounded by mystery, magic, and grace every day of our lives. Knowing you has brought all of those together into a dream of a future I never imagined. Thank you for allowing me to be a part of your world."

Again, the professor nodded before straightening up and taking on an official tone.

"Mist, do you take this man to honor and cherish, to love and care for, and to allow to read as much literature as he likes?"

"I do."

"Brilliant!" the professor said before continuing on. "And Michael, do you take this woman to honor and cherish, to love and care for, and to cook her remarkable meals not only for you but for all of us?"

"I do."

"Smashing! And now we have the rings."

Michael turned to Clay Jr. Lowering himself to the child's level, he loosened the ribbons on the velvet pillow and removed the rings. "Thank you for being such a great helper," he whispered.

Standing, he turned back to Mist, handing her the basic gold band they'd had Clive make. Mist slipped the gold band on Michael's ring finger. In turn, he did the same, gently sliding a narrow band that was sculpted to fit with the engagement ring he'd given her the Christmas before. With the ring exchange complete, they turned back to face the professor.

"Well now, I believe it's about time I say something like this: By the power so recently invested in me, I jolly well pronounce you husband and wife. Michael, I suggest you kiss the bride."

Which is exactly what Michael did as a round of applause broke out. After exchanging a heartfelt kiss, they faced the small audience. Mist was especially pleased to see Hollister watching from the back of the room. Michael took a bow, and Mist did a graceful curtsy. At which point, to Mist's surprise, Michael eased her back to face the floral arch and picture window.

As the bride and groom turned, a tiny light went on outside, like a firefly but brighter. Then another light flickered. And another. One by one, a sea of lights grew across the front yard until it became clear that they were candles held by people, dozens—no, hundreds—of people. Mist grabbed Michael's hand and pulled him toward the front door. Throwing it open, she gasped. Townsfolk covered the lawn, spilled out onto the sidewalk, and filled the street.

Mist and Michael stepped out on the porch and the crowd cheered, shouting congratulations and wishes for a bright future together. Mist felt tears well up at the unexpected outpouring of love from the community.

Feeling a hand touch her elbow, she turned to find Maisie gesturing to a lengthy table on the porch. A tiered wedding cake graced one end of the table, its traditional style adorned with winter greenery and red berries. A sheet cake larger than she'd ever seen accompanied it, ready to be shared with all.

"This is how much you are loved," Michael said, putting his arm around Mist's shoulder to pull her close. "This is your family, the people you feed, the community that is grateful for all you do for them. You are a blessing to this town."

"They are a blessing to me," Mist whispered, barely able to get the words out in view of the town's overwhelming gesture.

"How about cutting that cake?" The shouted suggestion came from the easily recognized voice of Wild Bill.

"A great idea," Michael said. "It's going to take some time to pass it out!" He and Mist approached the long table, and after the requisite cake-cutting and initial first-taste tradition—the groom being quite polite about it while the bride impishly missed her new husband's mouth by the tiniest bit—servings of wedding cake found the way to all corners of the front property and out into the street.

The winter temperature and late hour dictated a short celebration. So it was that, after many well wishes, only the wedding party and close friends remained, relaxing in the front parlor. Betty began to unobtrusively pick up cake plates, taking small trips to the kitchen. And Mist, finally sensing exhaustion set in after the long day, prepared to say good night and accompany Michael to their new home.

That was when Maisie made a sudden declaration. "Mist, you never threw your bouquet!"

"You're right, I didn't." Mist picked up her bouquet, admiring the beautiful multicolored cluster that Maisie had made for her.

"Well now," the professor said, "there's no time like the present."

Maisie swirled her hand, gesturing for Mist to turn around. Not one to disappoint, Mist turned and tossed the floral arrangement over her head at a haphazard angle, where it sailed freely, ribbons trailing through the air. Which is when Betty happened to walk back in the room to find the bouquet land in her arms.

Surprised, she looked around, eyebrows raised. Her gaze came to rest on Clive, who shrugged his shoulders, sauntered over, and surprised everyone with his next words:

"Why not?"

NINETEEN

As firmly suggested by Betty, Clive, and just about everyone else, Mist and Michael arrived at Christmas-morning breakfast as it was getting underway. Applause from those already at tables greeted them when they entered. Betty and Clive popped out of the kitchen at the sound.

"I thought we told you two to be *late* to breakfast," Clive called out from across the café. He waved a spatula in the air as a faux reprimand.

"This is the best we could do." Michael shrugged his shoulders and grinned. "*Someone* insisted on seeing how breakfast was coming along." He wrapped one arm around Mist's shoulders and pulled her into a side hug. She escaped quickly, gave him a kiss, and headed across the café. She slipped past Clive and into the kitchen. Betty followed, but Clive lingered to double-check a breakfast order from Hannah and Alex.

"What was it you youngins ordered again?"

"An alligator!" Alex exclaimed.

"A turtle!" Hannah said.

"You got it!" Clive turned away and disappeared into the kitchen, joining Mist and Betty.

"Well now, married lady," Clive said as he took a place in front of a griddle. "Would you and that husband of yours like any exotic hotcakes? Alligators and turtles are on special today." He grabbed a pitcher and poured batter into surprisingly realistic animal shapes. A bowl of raisins sat nearby, ready to provide eyes for creatures in need.

"I'll take a dragonfly," Mist said, at first teasing, then realizing a pancake sounded delicious. Had she eaten the day before? She vaguely remembered making a plate of salad.

"Make that a moose for me," Michael said, leaning in the doorway. "Unless you need help, I'll be sitting with Nigel." Seeing Clive wave him away, he disappeared into the café.

Mist turned to Betty. "Thank you for all this!"

"Pfft! Christmas-morning breakfast is easy," Betty reminded her. "It's only hotel guests, and I swear people are always still full from the big dinner the night before. Not to mention the cake! My, my, wasn't that something?"

"I was wondering about that," Mist said. "How on earth did you pull that off?"

Clive flipped an alligator in the air and answered, "Clayton picked the cakes up in Helena the day before. He stored the tall one in the firehouse fridge. And that huge sheet cake was stored in four quarters, one each with Millie, Marge, Sally, and Glenda. They pieced it together when we set everything up on the porch."

"Amazing," Mist said. "You're all amazing."

She joined Michael in the café. Thirty minutes, one moose, and one dragonfly later, breakfast wrapped up, and the group moved to the front parlor while Mist retrieved the miniature paintings she'd made for the guests. She met back up with everyone near the Christmas tree, which had been returned to its prime location in front of the picture window, the floral arch now relocated to the corner. She slipped the miniature paintings, wrapped in rice paper and raffia, under the tree.

Dancing flames glowed in the fireplace, thanks to a fire Clive had built early in the morning. Hannah and Alex opened gifts their parents had brought with them. Clive, per annual tradition, gave Betty a hand-crafted silver ornament to add to the collection he'd created for her over the years. Together, they hung the sweet design, the script word *joy*, on the tree as tiny Yogo sapphires embedded in the lettering sparkled under the light.

Mist took the wrapped mini paintings and distributed them to the hotel guests. "It is our tradition to give you something to take with you as a remembrance of your holiday here. I hope these will bring you good memories in the future."

Bits of wrapping fell to the side as each guest found the treasure inside.

"This is beautiful!" Elaine exclaimed, holding up her painting. "Now I have a Christmas Joy basket to take home with me!"

"So do I!" Hannah squealed. "And it has lots of things in it, including cocoa!"

"You helped me make those cocoa packets," Mist said. "It seemed only fair you should get to have one."

"Just don't try to mix it with water," Burton advised.

"Don't be silly, Dad." Hannah laughed.

Burton smiled. "It's my New Year's resolution to be sillier, so you might have to get used to it."

"It's a good resolution," Elaine whispered. She patted Burton on the knee.

"My friend's red truck is in my basket! Cool!" Alex said.

"Ours are filled with flowers," Rose said, holding hers up as Violet did the same.

"They're lovely," Violet agreed.

"Thank you, Mist," the professor said, showing his painted basket filled with books. Instead of a ribbon on his basket, it boasted a red bow tie.

Mist and Michael exchanged smiles, having decided early on not to exchange gifts. They would fill their new home with many over time.

Clive clapped his hands. "Who's up for a snowball fight?"

"I am!" Alex jumped up and ran for his jacket.

"Count me in!" Violet stood up and followed.

One by one, each guest decided to participate, and soon snowballs flew in every direction. Even townsfolk passing by joined in.

Mist, Michael, Betty, and Clive threw a few snowballs themselves, then stood on the porch, watching the others. They exchanged glances, an unspoken agreement that this Christmas was indeed special.

It was then that Mist felt a sense of imminent change wash over her. For all that she believed time was fluid, that there was only "now," this felt different, the sense of an unexpected future just around the corner. The thought filled her with wonder, and a giddiness overtook her that caused her to giggle aloud. For her life had taken a direction that she'd never dreamed of or perhaps never even dared to hope for. When she thought back to the days after graduating from the university, trying to envision her future, how could she have known she would find a welcoming, nurturing community hidden away in the mountains of Montana? That she'd be able to create art and cuisine to feed her soul, that she'd find love and a future that promised new adventures. That, in Timberton, she would find joy.

BETTY'S COOKIE
EXCHANGE RECIPES

Glazed Cinnamon Nuts
Christmas Hugs and Kisses Cookies
Peppermint Snowball Cookies
Peanut Butter Cocoa Drops
Gluten-Free Apple Cookies
No-Bake Gluten-Free Cookies
Raspberry Bars
Easy Pudding Cookies
Coconut Oatmeal Cookies
Hearty Banana Tea Loaves/Muffins
Double-Chocolate Lemon Cookies
Mocha Peppermint Cookies
Cranberry Almond Scone Cookies
Mexican Wedding Cakes
Banana Oatmeal Cookies
Lila's Lace Cookies
Holly Cookies
Chocolate Waffle Cookies
Frosted Sugar Cookies
Chocolate Crinkle Cookies
Easy Peanut Butter Cookies
Chocolate-Dipped Shortbread Cookies
Cranberry Orange Cookies
Raspberry Almond Cookies
Cranberry Walnut Pinwheels
Mini Cranberry Tarts

Glazed Cinnamon Nuts
(a family recipe)

Ingredients:

1 cup sugar
1/4 cup water
1/8 teaspoon cream of tartar
Heaping teaspoon of cinnamon
1 tablespoon butter
1-1/2 cups walnut halves

Directions:

Boil sugar, water, cream of tartar, and cinnamon to soft boil stage (236°).

Remove from heat.

Add butter and walnuts.

Stir until walnuts separate.

Place on waxed paper to cool.

CHRISTMAS HUGS AND KISSES COOKIES

(Submitted by Kim Davis of *Cinnamon and Sugar and a Little Bit of Murder* blog)

Ingredients:

1 cup all-purpose flour
1/2 cup unsweetened cocoa powder
1/2 teaspoon salt
1/2 cup unsalted butter, room temperature
2/3 cup granulated sugar
1 egg
1/2 teaspoon peppermint extract
3/4 cup holiday-themed nonpareils and jimmies (use a mixture)
24 Hershey's Hugs and Kisses candies, unwrapped (or a combination of the two)

Directions:

In a medium bowl, whisk together the flour, cocoa powder, and salt.

Using an electric mixer, beat the butter on medium-high speed until creamy.

Add in the sugar and beat for 2 minutes until light and fluffy. Beat in the egg and the peppermint extract until thoroughly combined.

Refrigerate the dough for at least 30 minutes.
Preheat the oven to 350°. Line two baking sheets with parchment paper and set aside.

Place the sprinkles in a shallow dish. Shape the dough into balls about the size of a small walnut and roll in the sprinkles. Place on baking sheet at least 2 inches apart.

Bake cookies, one sheet at a time, for 10 to 11 minutes. Remove the pan from the oven and lightly press a Hugs and Kiss candy into the center of each cookie while they are warm.

Allow cookies to rest on baking sheet for 5 minutes, then remove to a wire rack to cool before eating.

Let Hugs and Kisses firm up before storing in an airtight container for up to one week.

Tip:

Use different-colored sprinkles for other holidays and special occasions.

Peppermint Snowball Cookies
(Submitted by Shelia Hall)

Ingredients:

2 cups + 2 tablespoons all-purpose flour
2 teaspoon cornstarch
1 cup salted sweet cream butter softened
3 cups powdered sugar divided (2 cups and 1 cup)
1 teaspoon pure peppermint extract
1/2 teaspoon pure vanilla extract
1-1/4 cup mini semisweet chocolate chips
5–6 drops hot pink/rose food color gel
1/4 cup finely crushed peppermint candies

Directions:

Whisk together the flour and cornstarch. Set it aside.

Using either a stand mixer or a large mixing bowl and a handheld mixer on medium-high, beat the softened butter for 30 seconds. Add the 1 cup of powdered sugar and beat for another 1 to 1-1/2 minutes.

Lower the mixer speed to medium-low, add in the peppermint and vanilla extracts. Keeping the mixer speed on medium-low, add in the flour mixture. Mix just until the ingredients are well incorporated. Increase the mixer speed to medium and add the red food color. Mix just until the color is uniform.

Add in the mini chocolate chips and mix just until combined and well distributed. Cover the dough and chill in the refrigerator for 10 minutes.

Preheat the oven to 350°F. Line two baking sheets with parchment paper, one for baking the dough balls and one for the rolled cookies to finish cooling on. Set them aside.

Using a 1 tablespoon cookie dough scoop, scoop out the cookie dough. Roll the dough into a ball and place on the prepared baking sheet. Space the rolled cookie dough balls 1 inch apart. Bake for 10–12 minutes.

Add the remaining 2 cups powdered sugar and the crushed peppermint candies to a medium-size mixing bowl. Whisk to combine. Set it aside.

Remove the cookies from the oven and allow them to rest on the cookie sheet for 5 minutes. Roll the cookies in the powdered sugar mixture. Transfer the coated cookies to the second prepared cookie sheet.

PEANUT BUTTER COCOA DROPS
(Submitted by Shelia Hall)

Ingredients:

2 cups sugar
1/3 cup unsweetened cocoa powder
1/2 cup milk
1 stick of butter
1 teaspoon vanilla
Pinch of salt
1/2 cup peanut butter (chunky)
2 cups quick-cooking oats

Directions:

Combine the sugar, cocoa milk, and butter in a medium saucepan. Cook on medium heat until it comes to a boil, stirring occasionally.

Boil for 1 minute. Remove from heat and stir in the vanilla, salt, peanut butter, and oats.

Drop by rounded spoonfuls onto waxed paper or aluminum foil.

Cool for around an hour, then store in an airtight container.

GLUTEN-FREE APPLE COOKIES
(Submitted by Petrenia Etheridge)

Ingredients:

4 packets apple instant oatmeal
1/2 cup sugar
1/4 cup butter, softened
1 tablespoon honey
1 teaspoon vanilla
1/2 teaspoon cinnamon
1/4 teaspoon salt
1 large egg

Directions:

Cream together butter and sugar. Add in everything except oatmeal and mix well. Then stir in oatmeal and mix well.

Spoon onto greased cookie sheet by teaspoon size. No need to flatten.

Bake at 350 for 10 min. They will have a chewy texture. For crisper cookies, add 1/2 cup gluten-free flour.

NO-BAKE GLUTEN-FREE COOKIES
(Submitted by Petrenia Etheridge)

Ingredients:

1/2 cup butter
2 cup sugar
4 tablespoons cocoa
1/2 cup peanut butter
1/2 cup milk
1 tablespoon corn syrup
Pinch salt
1 teaspoon vanilla
3 cups quick oats

Directions:

In saucepan, melt butter. Add cocoa powder, sugar, salt, corn syrup, and milk. Stir until smooth.

Once boiling, boil for 2-1/2 minutes and remove from heat.

Stir in peanut butter and vanilla, then fold in oats.

Spoon onto parchment paper to cool.

Raspberry Bars
(Submitted by Brenda Ellis)

Ingredients:

One box yellow cake mix
2-1/2 cups quick oats
3/4 cup melted butter
12 oz. jar raspberry preserves

Directions:

Combine cake mix and oats. Stir in butter and mix until crumbly.

Press about 3 cups into a 9 x 13 pan.

Spread raspberry (or other fruit) preserves over mixture.

Sprinkle remaining crumb mixture over preserves. Pat gently to level.

Bake at 375° for 24–26 minutes. Cool completely and cut into bars.

EASY PUDDING COOKIES
(Submitted by Jan Knight)

Ingredients:

1/2 cup butter (softened)
1/2 cup sugar
1 pkg (3.9 oz.) dry instant pudding mix (see note below)
2 eggs
1-1/2 cups flour
1/2 teaspoon baking soda
1/4 teaspoon salt

Directions:

Mix in order given.

I usually add 1–3 Tablespoons liquid, such as milk, to make the dough the right consistency.

Drop by spoonfuls on greased baking sheet.

Bake at 350° till done.

Frost or not, whatever you wish.

Tip: Any flavor pudding can be used. I like chocolate with nuts or frosted. For Christmas, you could top with chopped candy canes. Other flavors include lemon, white chocolate… just use your imagination! Enjoy!

COCONUT OATMEAL COOKIES
(Submitted by Linda Bye)

Ingredients:

1 cup of softened butter
1/4 cup white sugar
3/4 cup packed brown sugar
2 eggs
1 teaspoon baking soda
1 small package of coconut cream instant jello pudding
1-1/4 cup flour
1 cup old-fashioned oats
2-1/2 cups quick oats

Directions:

Blend together butter and sugars until smooth.

Add eggs, baking soda, and pudding package.

Mix in flour and all oats.

With a tablespoon, distribute dough on 2 nonstick 18 x 13 cookie sheets.

Bake 9–11 minutes at 375°.

Recipe makes approx. 48 cookies.

Optional add-ins:
1 cup craisins
1 cup of semisweet chocolate chips

Hearty Banana Tea Loaves/Muffins
(Submitted by Jennifer Harvey)

Ingredients:

1/2 cup boiling water
1 cup rolled oats
1-1/2 cups mashed bananas (approx. 3 medium)
1 cup brown sugar
2 eggs
1 teaspoon vanilla
1-1/3 cups flour
2 teaspoons baking soda
1/4 teaspoon salt

Directions:

Preheat oven to 350° for loaves or 400° for muffins.

Butter pans or dust with flour. Cupcake liners may be used to line muffin pans.

Pour boiling water over oats to soften. Let cool.

Mix bananas, sugar, eggs, and vanilla in a large mixing bowl. Add flour, soda, salt, and softened oats to banana mixture.

Beat until smooth. Add batter to prepared pans.

Bake tea loaves for approx. 40 minutes at 350°.
Bake muffins for 15–25 minutes at 400°.

Bread is done when inserted toothpick comes out clean.

Optional: Sprinkle tops with turbinado sugar and walnut pieces for a lovely crunch.

DOUBLE-CHOCOLATE LEMON COOKIES
(Submitted by Lanette Fields)

Ingredients:

2 sticks of butter or Earth Balance, softened
1 teaspoon vanilla
2 eggs or egg substitute
2 cups dark brown sugar, packed.
2/3 cup baking cocoa
3 cups of one-to-one gluten-free flour with xanthan gum
1-1/2 teaspoon baking soda
1 teaspoon of baking powder
1 bag of semisweet chocolate chips
Zest of one large lemon

Directions:

Preheat oven to 325° on convection bake.

Sift together flour, cocoa, baking soda, and baking powder. Set aside.

Mix butter, sugar, eggs, and vanilla until well combined.

Add dry ingredients slowly to creamed mixture just until completely blended.

Add one bag of semisweet chocolate chips.

Add the zest of one large lemon.

Mix until incorporated.

Use cookie scoop or make cookie balls about size of walnuts. Put on parchment-lined baking sheets about three fingers apart.

Bake about 10 minutes or until desired doneness. Let them cool on baking sheet or after one minute transfer to cooling racks to cool.

Makes about 43 cookies.

Tips: When cool, wrap cookies in plastic wrap and put in freezer bag to stay fresh longer. Can be stored in the freezer for about 6 months. Regular flour can be substituted for gluten-free flour and real butter for buttery sticks. Amount of flour and leveling may need to be adjusted. Use chocolate chips such as Guittard 46% Cacao chips for nondairy.

MOCHA PEPPERMINT COOKIES
(Submitted by Colleen Galster)

Ingredients:

1 box gluten-free chocolate cake mix (I use King Arthur brand)
2 eggs
1/3 cup melted butter
1 teaspoon peppermint extract
2 teaspoons peppermint coffee creamer or other holiday flavors. You can use milk instead if you prefer.
1 cup semisweet chocolate chips
1 cup white chocolate chips
Peppermint baking chips or crushed candy canes optional
Butterscotch chips (optional)
Caramel syrup (optional)

Directions:

Preheat oven to 350°.
In a large mixing bowl, add the eggs, and beat slightly.

Stir in the cake mix, melted butter, peppermint extract and coffee creamer or milk, and mix until well combined.

Stir in the chocolate and white chocolate chips.

Drop by rounded tablespoonful onto cookie sheet, leaving about 2 inches between cookies.

Place several peppermint chips/candy cane pieces and chocolate chips on top of each cookie.

Bake for 8 to 10 minutes or until edges are slightly firm.

Remove from oven and allow to cool completely.
Drizzle with caramel syrup if desired.

Cranberry Almond Scone Cookies
(Submitted by Molly Elliott)

Ingredients:

1/2 cup butter, softened (1 stick)
1/3 cup granulated sugar
1/3 cup brown sugar
1 teaspoon vanilla
1 egg (or egg replacer)
1 1/2 cups all-purpose flour
1/2 teaspoon baking powder
1/4 teaspoon baking soda
1/2 teaspoon salt
2 tablespoons milk
1/2 cup dried cranberries
1/2 cup sliced almonds

Directions:

Sift dry ingredients together and set aside.

Cream butter and sugar together. Add vanilla and egg (or egg replacer).

Add dry ingredients and milk. Mix well.

Add cranberries and sliced almonds (or additions of choice).

Mix and drop by spoonful on greased baking sheet. Press cookies down slightly before putting in the oven.

Bake approx. 10 minutes at 350°.

MEXICAN WEDDING CAKES
(Submitted by Betty Escobar)

Ingredients:

2 cups butter
1 cup confectioners sugar (plus extra)
1 teaspoon vanilla
4 cups flour
1 cup finely chopped pecans

Directions:

Preheat oven to 350°.

Cream butter and one cup confectioners' sugar until light and fluffy, 5–7 minutes. Beat in vanilla.

Gradually beat in flour and stir in pecans.

Shape tablespoons of dough into 2-inch crescents.

Bake 12–15 minutes or until light brown.

Roll in additional confectioners' sugar while warm.
Cool on wire racks.

BANANA OATMEAL COOKIES
(Submitted by M.J. McKinniss, from Gramma R.)

Ingredients:

1/2 cup sugar
1/2 cup brown sugar
2 eggs beaten
1 cup shortening
2 cups sifted flour
2 cups oatmeal—not cooked
1 cup mashed bananas
1 teaspoon baking soda
1 teaspoon vanilla
One bag of butterscotch chips (10 or 12 oz. bag)

Directions:

Sift flour into mixing bowl, add the rest of the ingredients and mix until well blended.

Add the entire bag of butterscotch chips or only as many as you'd like.

Bake at 375°on a greased cookie sheet for about 12 minutes or until golden brown.

An alternate to the butterscotch chips:

My grandmother originally made these cookies with date fruits (pits removed). The batter for this cookie is thick, so you can take a date fruit, just one, and put it on the underside of the tablespoon or so of cookie dough, slightly pushing it into the dough (this would be the bottom of the cookie when done). I put the date on the cookie sheet, then put my blob of cookie dough on top of it and kind of form it around the date. The date will caramelize while baking.

LILA'S LACE COOKIES
(Submitted by Sallie Reynolds, from Lila Doggett)

Ingredients:

1 cup melted butter
2 cups brown sugar
1 large egg
1 teaspoon vanilla
1 cup pecan meats
2 cups rolled oats

Directions:

Mix ingredients in order given.

Drop by teaspoonful, placing far apart on baking sheet.

Bake 5-7 minutes at 375°.

Let the cookies cool thoroughly.

HOLLY COOKIES
(Submitted by Betty Escobar)

Ingredients:

1/2 cup butter
30 large (not jumbo) marshmallows
1/2 teaspoon vanilla
1-1/2 teaspoons green food coloring
3-1/2 cups cornflakes
Red cinnamon candies

Directions:

In large pot, melt butter and marshmallows together, stirring constantly.

Add vanilla and food coloring.

Stir in cornflakes.

Drop spoonfuls with a greased spoon onto a greased cookie sheet or wax paper sprayed with vegetable oil.

Place 2 cinnamon candies on each bunch of holly, pressing lightly to make sure they stick.

Let sit until they set.

Note: To make these gluten-free, make sure to use brands of marshmallows and cornflakes that are gluten-free.

CHOCOLATE WAFFLE COOKIES
(Submitted by Vera Kenyon)

Ingredients:

1-1/2 cups sugar
1 cup butter
4 eggs
2 teaspoons vanilla
2 cups flour
8 tablespoons cocoa
Dash of salt

Directions:

Cream sugar and butter. Beat in eggs and vanilla.

Mix in dry ingredients.

Place a spoonful of batter in each section of your waffle iron. Bake a minute or two.

Remove the waffles, let cool and add frosting and sprinkles if you like.

Frosted Sugar Cookies
(Submitted by Tracy Fritts)

Ingredients:

Cookie dough:
1 cup unsalted butter softened
1 cup granulated sugar
1 ½ teaspoons vanilla extract
1 large egg
2 ½ cups all-purpose flour
¾ teaspoon baking powder
¾ teaspoon table salt

Sugar cookie frosting:
3 cups powdered sugar, sifted
4 tablespoons milk
2 tablespoons light corn syrup
½ teaspoon vanilla extract
Gel food coloring (optional)
Additional candies and sprinkles for decorating (optional)

Directions:

Sift flour, baking powder, and salt. Set aside.

Cream butter and sugar together.

Add vanilla and egg.

Add dry ingredients and mix. Chill for two hours.

Roll out cookie dough and cut into shapes with cookie cutters.

Bake approx. 10 minutes at 350 degrees. Allow to cool.

Mix frosting ingredients and decorate as desired.

CHOCOLATE CRINKLE COOKIES
(Submitted by Alisha Collins)

Ingredients:

1/2 cup unsweetened cocoa powder
1 cup white granulated sugar
1/4 cup vegetable oil
2 large eggs
2 teaspoons pure vanilla extract
1 cup all-purpose or plain flour
1 teaspoon baking powder
1/2 teaspoon salt
1/4 cup confectioner's sugar or icing sugar (for coating)

Directions:

In a medium-sized bowl, mix together the cocoa powder, white sugar, and vegetable oil. Beat in eggs one at a time until fully incorporated. Mix in the vanilla.

In another bowl, combine the flour, baking powder, and salt. Stir the dry ingredients into the wet mixture just until a dough forms. Do not over beat.

Cover bowl with wrap and refrigerate for at least 4 hours or overnight.

When ready to bake, preheat oven to 350°. Line 2 cookie sheets or baking trays with parchment paper.

Roll 1 tablespoonful of dough into balls for smaller cookies (or 2 tablespoonfuls for larger cookies).

Add the confectioners' sugar to a smaller bowl. Generously and evenly coat each ball of dough in confectioners' sugar and place onto prepared cookie sheets.

Bake in preheated oven for 10 minutes (for small cookies) or 12 minutes (for larger cookies). The cookies will come out soft from the oven but will harden up as they cool.

Allow to cool on the cookie sheet for 5 minutes before transferring to wire racks to cool.

EASY PEANUT BUTTER COOKIES
(Submitted by Alisha Collins)

Ingredients:

1 cup peanut butter
1 cup sugar
1 egg

Directions:

Preheat oven to 350° and spray your pan with nonstick spray.

Combine all ingredients and drop by spoonfuls onto baking pan. Use a fork dipped in sugar to make the crisscross pattern.

Bake for 6–8 minutes only! They will be soft and barely brown on the bottom.

Option: Add peanut butter chips or dark chocolate chips.

CHOCOLATE-DIPPED SHORTBREAD COOKIES
(Submitted by Alisha Collins)

Ingredients:

1 cup salted butter, cold and cut up into pieces
2/3 cup granulated sugar
1 teaspoon almond extract (if you'd prefer the nut taste to be milder, use vanilla extract)
1/2 cup pecan pieces (I put mine in the food processor to get them nice and small)
2-1/4 cups all-purpose flour
1/2 cup Nutella
1/4 cup semisweet chocolate chips
2 tablespoons milk
1 tablespoon confectioners' sugar

Directions:

In the bowl of an electric mixer, cream butter and sugar. Add in almond (or vanilla) extract. When these ingredients are well blended, add pecan pieces.

Gradually add flour and mix at low speed until combined, then increase speed to medium until your dough is no longer sandy-looking.

Put a piece of parchment paper on a baking tray and turn dough out of mixing bowl. Divide in half. Form each half into a rectangle. I use my thumb as a width guide. Cover with plastic wrap and chill for 1 hour.

Preheat oven to 350°.

Unwrap dough and use a pizza cutter to cut into sticks. Keep sticks close together on tray so they don't spread.

Bake in preheated oven for 15–20 minutes or until shortbread is golden and semifirm to the touch.

Cool completely.

Over a double boiler, melt the semisweet chocolate chips, milk, sugar, and Nutella until smooth. You can also use a glass bowl in the microwave. Just make sure the chocolate doesn't burn.

Dip your shortbread sticks into the chocolate-Nutella mixture. Let cookies harden on parchment paper or just gobble them up there and then.

CRANBERRY ORANGE COOKIES
(Submitted by Patti Rusk)

Cookie dough:
1 cup unsalted butter, softened
1 cup white sugar
1/2 cup packed brown sugar
1 large egg
2 tablespoons orange juice
1 teaspoon grated orange zest
2-1/2 cups all-purpose flour
1/2 teaspoon baking soda
1/2 teaspoon salt
2 cups chopped cranberries or craisins
1/2 cup chopped walnuts

Glaze:
1-1/2 cups confectioners' sugar
3 tablespoons orange juice
1/2 teaspoon grated orange zest

Directions:

Preheat oven to 375°.

Cream butter, white sugar, and brown sugar in a mixing bowl until smooth. Beat in egg until well blended. Mix in orange juice and zest.

Whisk together flour, baking soda, and salt in a separate bowl. Stir flour mixture into the butter mixture until combined. Mix in cranberries and walnuts.

Drop dough by rounded tablespoonfuls 2 inches apart onto ungreased cookie sheets.

Bake in the preheated oven 11–14 minutes until edges are golden brown. Be sure to turn racks halfway through.

Cool cookies completely before adding glaze.

To make the glaze:
Mix together confectioners' sugar, orange juice, and zest in a small bowl until smooth.

Drizzle or spread glaze over the tops of the cooled cookies. Let stand until set.

Raspberry Almond Cookies
(Submitted by Patti Rusk)

Ingredients:

1 cup butter, softened
2/3 cup white sugar
1-1/4 teaspoons almond extract, divided
2 cups all-purpose flour
1/2 cup seedless raspberry jam
1/2 cup confectioners' sugar
1 teaspoon milk

Directions:

Preheat the oven to 350°.

Cookie dough:

Beat butter and white sugar together in a medium bowl until creamy. Mix in 1/2 teaspoon almond extract. Add flour and mix until dough comes together.

Form dough into 1-1/2-inch balls and place on ungreased cookie sheets about 2 inches apart.

Use your thumb or back of measuring spoon to press down and make a dent in the center of each ball. Fill with jam.

Bake until edges are lightly browned, about 14 to 18 minutes; allow to cool on cookie sheet for a few minutes.

Drizzle:
Mix confectioners' sugar, milk, and remaining 3/4 teaspoon almond extract together in a medium bowl until smooth; drizzle lightly over warm cookies.

CRANBERRY WALNUT PINWHEEL COOKIES
(Submitted by Cecile VanTyne)

Ingredients:

1 cup of dried cranberries, chopped
1 cup of chopped walnuts
1/2 cup of sugar
Zest of one orange
2 refrigerated pie crusts
2 tablespoons of butter, melted
1 tablespoon of butter for filling
1 whole egg
2 tablespoons of water
Honey

Directions:

Preheat oven to 400°.

Line a baking sheet with parchment paper and set aside.

In a pot, add cranberries, walnuts, sugar, orange zest and one tablespoon of butter until warm. Let it cool while doing the next step.

On a lightly floured surface, roll out the pie crusts into two squares.

Brush the pie crusts generously with two tablespoons of melted butter.

Spread the cooled filling onto the pie crusts. Don't overfill. Roll each pie crust into a log. Pinch the edges to seal.

Put egg and water into a small bowl and beat with a fork until combined.

Brush each log with the egg mixture.

Cut each log into ten pieces. Might want to freeze them for ten minutes to make the slicing easier.

Place on baking sheet about 1 inch apart.

Bake for 12–15 minutes or until golden brown.

Let cool on a rack.

Drizzle a teaspoon or more of honey on each pinwheel.

Mini Cranberry Tarts
(Submitted by Cecile VanTyne)

Ingredients:

Cinnamon sugar
1 box of puff pastry
1 cup of cranberry sauce
Butter, melted

Directions:

Preheat oven to 400 degrees and grease a cupcake pan.

If you don't already have some made, mix together some cinnamon and sugar to your liking.

Unroll puff pastry and sprinkle with the cinnamon sugar. Press gently into the dough.

Cut each puff pastry sheet into nine squares and fill each square with no more than two teaspoons of cranberry sauce. Pick up the square by the corners using your thumbs and index fingers, pinching them together as you're putting them in the cupcake pan. Sprinkle them with more cinnamon sugar.

Bake for 25–30 minutes until golden brown.

Serve cooled or warm with whipped cream or ice cream. You can also sprinkle with powdered sugar.

RECIPE NOTES

RECIPE NOTES

RECIPE NOTES

Recipe Notes

Acknowledgments

Joy at Moonglow only exists because of the efforts of many. I owe immense gratitude to Annie Sarac for her outstanding editing and developmental guidance. Jay Garner, Karen Putnam, Elizabeth Christy, Carol Anderson, and Sallie Reynolds all deserve praise for beta reading and keen feedback. Kudos go to Matt and Judy Montagne for making sure Clara and Andrew have an excellent, fictional vacation in Hawaii. Lego Normarie and Tara Meyers deserve credit for formatting. And the beautiful cover design is by the very talented Mariah Sinclair.

There are many people in my life who help keep the spirit of Christmas alive in the Moonglow Christmas books. I thank Paul Sterrett for his continued patience as I pace the house each year, muttering plot points and character traits. And the Georgetown Writers deserve a huge round of applause for their support and encouragement.

Betty's cookie exchange is always a highlight of Christmas at the Timberton Hotel. The delicious recipes in this year's book are thanks to Kim Davis and her blog, *Cinnamon and Sugar and a Little Bit of Murder*, Petrenia Etheridge, Shelia Hall, Jennifer Harvey, Brenda Ellis, Linda Bye, Sallie Reynolds, Lanette Fields, Jan Knight, M. J. McKinniss, Colleen Galster, Alisha Collins, Vera Kenyon, Tracy Fritts, Cecile VanTyne, Patti Rusk, and Betty Escobar. Grab an apron, get baking, and enjoy!

BOOKS BY DEBORAH GARNER

The Paige MacKenzie Series

Above the Bridge

When NY reporter Paige MacKenzie arrives in Jackson Hole, it's not long before her instincts tell her there's more than a basic story to be found in the popular, northwestern Wyoming mountain area. A chance encounter with attractive cowboy Jake Norris soon has Paige chasing a legend of buried treasure passed down through generations. Sidestepping a few shady characters who are also searching for the same hidden reward, she will have to decide who is trustworthy and who is not.

The Moonglow Café

The discovery of an old diary inside the wall of the historic hotel soon sends NY reporter Paige MacKenzie into the underworld of art and deception. Each of the town's residents holds a key to untangling more than one long-buried secret, from the hippie chick owner of a new age café to the mute homeless man in the town park. As the worlds of western art and sapphire mining collide, Paige finds herself juggling research, romance, and danger.

Three Silver Doves

The New Mexico resort of Agua Encantada seems a perfect destination for reporter Paige MacKenzie to combine work with well-deserved rest and relaxation. But when suspicious jewelry shows up on another guest, and the town's storyteller goes missing, Paige's R&R is soon redefined as restlessness and risk. Will an unexpected overnight trip to Tierra Roja Casino lead her to the answers she seeks, or are darker secrets lurking along the way?

Hutchins Creek Cache

When a mysterious 1920s coin is discovered behind the Hutchins Creek Railroad Museum in Colorado, Paige MacKenzie starts digging into four generations of Hutchins family history, with a little help from the Denver Mint. As legends of steam engines and coin mintage mingle, will Paige discover the true origin of the coin, or will she find herself riding the rails dangerously close to more than one long-hidden town secret?

Crazy Fox Ranch

As Paige MacKenzie returns to Jackson Hole, she has only two things on her mind: enjoy life with Wyoming's breathtaking Grand Tetons as the backdrop and spend more time with handsome cowboy Jake Norris as he prepares to open his guest ranch. But when a stranger's odd behavior leads her to research Western filming in the area—in particular, the movie *Shane*, will it simply lead to a freelance article for the *Manhattan Post*, or will it lead to a dangerous, hidden secret?

Sweet Sierra Gulch

Paige MacKenzie isn't convinced there's anything "sweet" about Sweet Sierra Gulch when she arrives in the small California Gold Rush town. Still, there's plenty of history as well as anticipated romance with her favorite cowboy, Jake Norris. But when the owner of the local café goes missing, Paige is determined to find out why. Will she uncover a dangerous secret in the town's old mining tunnels, or will curiosity land her in over her head?

The Sadie Kramer Flair Series

A Flair for Chardonnay

When flamboyant senior sleuth Sadie Kramer learns the owner of her favorite chocolate shop is in trouble, she heads for the California wine country with a tote-bagged Yorkie and a slew of questions. The fourth generation Tremiato Winery promises answers, but not before a dead body turns up at the vintners' scheduled Harvest Festival. As Sadie juggles truffles, tips, and turmoil, she'll need to sort the grapes from the wrath in order to find the identity of the killer.

A Flair for Drama

When a former schoolmate invites Sadie Kramer to a theatre production, she jumps at the excuse to visit the Monterey Bay area for a weekend. Plenty of action is expected on stage, but when the show's leading lady turns up dead, Sadie finds herself faced with more than one drama to follow. With both cast members and production crew as potential suspects, will Sadie and her sidekick Yorkie, Coco, be able to solve the case?

A Flair for Beignets

With fabulous music, exquisite cuisine, and rich culture, how could a week in New Orleans be anything less than fantastic for Sadie Kramer and her sidekick Yorkie, Coco? And it is… until a customer at a popular patisserie drops dead face-first in a raspberry-almond tart. A competitive bakery, a newly formed friendship, and even her hotel's luxurious accommodations offer possible suspects. As Sadie sorts through a gumbo of interconnected characters, will she discover who the killer is, or will the killer discover her first?

A Flair for Truffles

Sadie Kramer's friendly offer to deliver three boxes of gourmet Valentine's Day truffles for her neighbor's chocolate shop backfires when she arrives to find the intended recipient deceased. Even more intriguing is the fact that the elegant heart-shaped gifts were ordered by three different men. With the help of one detective and the hindrance of another, Sadie will search San Francisco for clues. But will she find out "whodunit" before the killer finds a way to stop her?

A Flair for Flip-Flops

When the body of a heartthrob celebrity washes up on the beach outside Sadie Kramer's luxury hotel suite, her fun in the sun soon turns into sleuthing with the stars. The resort's wine and appetizer gatherings, suspicious guest behavior, and casual strolls along the beach boardwalk may provide clues, but will they be enough to discover who the killer is, or will mystery and mayhem leave a Hollywood scandal unsolved?

A Flair for Goblins

When Sadie Kramer agrees to help decorate for San Francisco's high-society Halloween shindig, she expects to find whimsical ghosts, skeletons, and jack-o-lanterns when she shows up at the Wainwright Mansion—not a body. With two detectives, a paranormal investigator turned television star, and a cauldron full of family members cackling around her, Sadie and her sidekick Yorkie are determined to find out who the killer is. Will an old superstition help lead to the truth? Or will this simply become one more tale in the mansion's haunted history?

The Moonglow Christmas Series

Mistletoe at Moonglow

The small town of Timberton, Montana, hasn't been the same since resident chef and artist, Mist, arrived, bringing a unique new age flavor to the old western town. When guests check in for the holidays, they bring along worries, fears, and broken hearts, unaware that Mist has a way of working magic in people's lives. One thing is certain: no matter how cold winter's grip is on each guest, no one leaves Timberton without a warmer heart.

Silver Bells at Moonglow

Christmas brings an eclectic gathering of visitors and locals to the Timberton Hotel each year, guaranteeing an eventful season. Add in a hint of romance, and there's more than snow in the air around the small Montana town. When the last note of Christmas carols has faded away, the soft whisper of silver bells from the front door's wreath will usher guests and townsfolk back into the world with hope for the coming year.

Gingerbread at Moonglow

The Timberton Hotel boasts an ambiance of near-magical proportions during the Christmas season. As the aromas of ginger, cinnamon, nutmeg, and molasses mix with heartfelt camaraderie and sweet romance, holiday guests share reflections on family, friendship, and life. Will decorating the outside of a gingerbread house prove easier than deciding what goes inside?

Nutcracker Sweets at Moonglow

When a nearby theater burns down just before Christmas, cast members of *The Nutcracker* arrive at the Timberton Hotel with only a sliver of holiday joy. Camaraderie, compassion, and shared inspiration combine to help at least one hidden dream come true. As with every Christmas season, this year's guests will face the New Year with a renewed sense of hope.

Snowfall at Moonglow
As holiday guests arrive at the Timberton Hotel with hopes of a white Christmas, unseasonably warm weather hints at a less-than-wintery wonderland. But whether the snow falls or not, one thing is certain: with resident artist and chef, Mist, around, there's bound to be a little magic. No one ever leaves Timberton without renewed hope for the future.

Yuletide at Moonglow
When a Yuletide festival promises jovial crowds, resident artist and chef, Mist, knows she'll have her hands full. Between the legendary Christmas Eve dinner at the Timberton Hotel and this season's festival events, the unique magic of Christmas in this small Montana town offers joy, peace, and community to guests and townsfolk alike. As always, no one will return home without a renewed sense of hope for the future.

Starlight at Moonglow
As the Christmas holiday approaches, a blizzard threatens the peaceful ambiance that the Timberton Hotel usually offers its guests. Even resident artist and chef, Mist, known to work near miracles, has no control over the howling winds and heavy snowfall. But there's always a bit of magic in this small Montana town, and this year's storm may just find it's no match for heartfelt camaraderie, joyful inspiration, and sweet romance.

————

Joy at Moonglow

Each holiday season is unique in the small Montana town of Timberton. New and returning guests bring their dreams, cares, and worries, and always leave with lighter hearts and renewed hope for the future. But no season has ever been as special as this one. Because, to everyone's delight, wedding bells will be ringing. Thanks to the heartfelt efforts of many and no shortage of sweet romance, this year will be the most joyful of all.

Additional titles:

Cranberry Bluff

Molly Elliott's quiet life is disrupted when routine errands land her in the middle of a bank robbery. Accused and cleared of the crime, she flees both media attention and mysterious, threatening notes to run a bed-and-breakfast on the Northern California coast. Her new beginning is peaceful until five guests show up at the inn, each with a hidden agenda. As true motives become apparent, will Molly's past come back to haunt her, or will she finally be able to leave it behind?

Sweet Treats: Recipes from the Moonglow Christmas Series

Delicious recipes, including Glazed Cinnamon Nuts, Cherry Pecan Holiday Cookies, Chocolate Peppermint Bark, Cranberry Drop Cookies, White Christmas Fudge, Molasses Sugar Cookies, Lemon Crinkles, Spiced Apple Cookies, Swedish Coconut

Cookies, Double-Chocolate Walnut Brownies, Blueberry Oatmeal Cookies, Cocoa Kisses, Angel Crisp Cookies, Gingerbread Eggnog Trifle, Dutch Sour Cream Cookies, and more!

For more information on Deborah Garner's books:

Facebook: https://www.facebook.com/
deborahgarnerauthor
Twitter: https://twitter.com/PaigeandJake
Website: http://deborahgarner.com
Mailing list: http://bit.ly/deborahgarner